T0082651

The
LOST
LOVED
ONES

The LOST LOVED ONES

JOANNE
HERRMANN

THE LOST LOVED ONES

iUniverse books may be ordered through booksellers or by contacting:

iUniverse
1663 Liberty Drive
Bloomington, IN 47403
www.iuniverse.com
844-349-9409

ISBN: 978-1-6632-1747-9 (sc)
ISBN: 978-1-6632-1748-6 (e)

Library of Congress Control Number: 2021901712

Print information available on the last page.

iUniverse rev. date: 01/30/2021

CONTENTS

STORY SUMMARY

The Lost Loved Ones focuses on the tribulations of a Dakota family, Takota Wachinskapa, a scout, and his wife, Makawee Hantaywee, and their three children, Tasunke Paytah, Tokala Kohana, and Anpaytoo HanWi. They befriend a trapper, Jonathan Griswald, who is known to them as, "Troubled Spirit," and who tries to live along the Mississippi River where Polish immigrants also settle. The Trapper's presence is pivotal, for without him, the family becomes stranded in a hostile community.

After the Dakota Uprising, The U.S. government imposed severe sanctions against the Natives: thirty eight of the men were hanged and the rest were arrested or banned from Minnesota under pain of death. The Dakota family was decimated. All except for the youngest son, Takota Kohana, who has left with Indigenous travelers only to return with a medicine man, Howahkan, to find his sister, Anpaytoo, HanWi, living among the settlers, who rename her Anya. He discovers why she has two children and that she is trying to cope with the settlers. Tokala Kohana and Howahkan take AnpaytooWi and her two children back with them to Canada where she can be reunited with the childhood love of her life, Chayton Enapay. Along the way, they experience the bountiful northeastern Minnesota wilderness in all its unspoiled, original abundance.

The story reveals the clash of two cultures: the Indigenous one of people who already lived in their "sacred" wilderness that they loved and cared for, and the Polish settlers, who, themselves, had lost their land in Europe and faced the hardships of a region that they tried to conquer and supplant with their "Old Country" ways on this achingly beautiful and terribly wild country that they adopted.

INTRODUCTORY STATEMENT

Be ready to be immersed in a legendary adventure with a Dakota family caught up in the turmoil of 1862. While the Civil War was raging along the East Coast, the Dakota Uprising broke out in the Minnesota heartland where the Great Sioux Nation clashed with settlers along the Minnesota and Mississippi River Valleys.

PROLOGUE

"I did not know then how much was ended. A people's dream died there. It was a beautiful dream." Black Elk, Lakota Medicine Man and Warrior

In the old days, my mother told me, this immense land was dense with forests, lakes, rivers and streams in territories claimed by over 500 nations. The woods were filled with four-legged and winged creatures, who lived with us off fruits, roots, vegetables, fish and game, all considered gifts from the Great Mystery, Wakan Tanka, which was why we honored everything as sacred. On a good day, we heard the trees whisper to each other and felt them share their fresh breath with us, and the sun sent its rays through the branches above, surrounding us below in a pool of light. The fragrant green thickets and undergrowth around us would rustle as we walked along the trail while the winged creatures chirped and chattered, and small four leggeds scampered on the tree limbs, where they could leap from tree to tree for miles on end. Wherever we walked we knew we were in a sacred place, and we were a living, breathing part of the life of the Creator, Wakan Tanka.

Still fresh in our memories were vast, plentiful forests overflowing with provisions where the markers were trails, rivers and lakes, teeming with fish, but, later, immoveable forts of the intruders emerged while our villages of tipis were moveable. Depending on where we camped and throughout the land when fruits were in season, our women could walk along the woodland paths and fill their reed baskets with honeyberries, strawberries, red mulberries, four kinds of currents, gooseberries, blueberries, wild raspberries, ground-cherries, wintergreen berries, checker berries, and Saskatoon berries that could be found on the prairies. Different tribes also grew plots of tomatoes, potatoes, maize, squash, and beans in this seemingly endless food forest.

At the edge of the woods, west of the great river, a prairie of tall rough grasses and flowering plants, many of them herbs, extended as far as the eye could see. If we rode into it, we soon saw the herds of dark, furry buffalo, lumbering like a shadow over the waves of the sea of prairie grass, a thundering storm of four leggeds, who lowered their horns on their shaggy heads and eyed us, while the ground trembled beneath us when they galloped past in a cloud that smelled of their sweat and swirled with dust. They knew why we pursued them, because they were wakan (sacred); they came to us to be our food, our clothing, and our shelter. This was our sacred, wakan pact.

We lived by the rivers and lakes where the waters were clear and purifying, the air was clean and fresh and shared with every living, growing thing. We were blessed with a sense of the sacred, with wakan and the Great Sacred Mystery, Wakan Tanka. We were the children of the land, who had arisen from its soil and returned to it through the birds of the air that replenished themselves on our departing bodies. We were the original people, and this land, Turtle Island, was ours.

Our ancestors to the East saw the invaders arrive on their large ships; They seemed to have lost their way across the great waters, and the members of the tribes wondered how the short, pale-faced ones could survive with what little they knew about the land. They called us "Indians" and took some of us with them across the big waters to places far away. Our travelers returned with stories about crowded cities, cluttered with wooden buildings leaning over stench filled walkways, crowded with bone-thin people in rags. From there they were escorted into huge stone palaces with throne rooms where men and women stood before a king and queen, all of them dressed in rich, lavish garments. Those of our ancestors who were able to return across the rough seas came to us with the terrifying news that these strangers must be crazy Wasi'chus, (greedy ones) because those, who had goods and riches, hoarded them and did not share them. They'd watched the fruit on the tree die, rather than share it, no matter what misery that caused.

The Wasi'chus returned again and again, bringing cattle, horses, pigs, chickens, metal knives, axes, and saws, iron kettles, guns with ammunition, glassware and their clothes made of cotton, linen and wool. Though we tried, there was no way we could stop them. They built their houses surrounded by a wooden wall, they called a stockade. Then they took everything they could find and destroyed it — entire sections of forests were felled, lands torn up with their plowing, streams diverted and filled with their refuse. Even though they stored their plentiful harvest in large bins, they began to look at us with the fierce eyes of hungry wolves. The savagery of these little hairy-faced men with their haggard women and the diseases they brought were unexpected, bloody and brutal.

So the fierce fight for survival erupted — on our side it was to honor the land, which sustained us and gave meaning to our lives; on their side, it was a chance to profit from its vast, abundant resources. Though we formed leagues to fight them when they broke our treaties, they fought back with a deadly fury. Though they agreed to stay east of the mountains they called the Appalachians, as soon as they were aware of the gold metal they craved in the West, they broke that treaty and claimed our territories. Even their Civil War didn't stop them from driving our Great Sioux nation of Dakotas, Lakotas and Nakotas out of the land of Minnesota which we had claimed for decades.

I am the son of Anpayto and this is our story.

Dakota Uprising, MN: 1862 to 1867 – (Civil War:
April 12, 1861 to May 9, 1865) The Sand Creek, CO
Massacre, The Red River TX War: 1864 to 1874

1

A REMNANT BREAKS AWAY

Shimmering were the waters of the great river, rippling with rings of light in the late afternoon sun. Living creatures receded deep into the stillness of the surrounding forest whenever there was the slightest disturbance. One that was almost imperceptible was moving upriver until the distant form emerged in the shape of a man rowing a canoe until he slowed, swerved, and headed toward the riverbank, accompanied by swirls of water that disappeared into the cold current.

There, with a series of splashes, he staggered out of the canoe, and pulled it through the waters, dragged it scraping onto the sandy shore and pushed it behind a scrub bush where he covered it with rustling branches. Tall, swarthy, bare-chested and sturdy, he could have been mistaken for a native if it weren't for the tattered breeches he wore. His scruffy long dark hair and stubby mustache seemed to blend in with the outgrowth from the towering embankment that he grabbed with gnarled hands while he climbed upward, grunting, his muscular arms straining and glistening with sweat while he gasped with the effort of heaving himself over the top, landing on brambles and branches with a thud where he rolled and lay back, his chest rising and falling, his body trembling with the strain of exhaustion. Staring up at the cobalt blue sky through the towering tree branches, he realized that he could go no further and drifted off into a deep sleep as the shadows of evening covered him. At times, he would moan unable to rest easy.

He awoke under a new moon, shrouded in darkness, lighted by the stars that glimmered through the moving clouds. When he pushed himself up from his nest of brambles, sharp thorns penetrated his hands, and the branches beneath him scraped his back and tore at his breeches, but he arose and stepped barefoot onto a latticework of undergrowth. With his scruffy hands outstretched, he felt his way around the trees and bushes, stumbled and grabbed a sapling. Turning, he leaned back feeling the bark scrape against his shoulders while he sank down with a sigh and sat beneath it. Something warm was running across his thick, gnarled fingers, which he lifted, smelled and tasted until he realized that blood was congealing on his large hands. Under cover of darkness, he dropped off again into a fitful sleep.

When he awoke with the dawn, he saw a clearing a few paces away, yet realized with a wry smile that creased his rugged, weather-beaten face that he could not have gone any further. Aware that he needed food and shelter, he wondered what life force kept him going, for he had lost everything, and where did he expect to find anything again? What drove him to stand? to work his way down the embankment where he squatted and pulled out the embedded thorns from his hands while he immersed them into the frigid, rushing, cleansing waters? Why, by mid morning, did he stand in the river with a hewn stick he used to spear a flopping fish, which he carried back with him to devour raw? Why did he spend the rest of the day foraging until he had a small pile of edible roots and berries lying in front of him in the middle of the clearing where he sat down to eat? Like a wild animal, he felt the grim, ruthless need to survive.

By nightfall, he had formed a bed of leafy boughs and covered himself with his buckskin jacket that he had retrieved from the canoe. Despite the night sounds of the howl of wolves in the distance, the grunt of bears, the hoot of owls and the scurry of countless unseen creatures; his rest was not fitful for he seemed to take comfort in the creatures living around him under the sliver of a crescent moon in the clearing that cradled him beneath the sheltering trees. But he awoke in the middle of the night and shuddered, arising and kneeling in his makeshift bed, remembering. A lament surfaced in his throat, a keening which arose to a wolf-like wail while he rocked back and forth. His wild cries of anguish shattered the silence, rising and falling like a chant, and then, dropped off into the eerie stillness of knowing that he was lost and alone.

Whatever life was out there was awakened, alerted, and watchful. The observers noticed that, after the first day when he used his starter kit to kindle a fire and his hunting knife to whittle down saplings and build a lean-to, he began to follow a routine. By then he had fashioned some make-shift tools. One of them was a long stick spear to harpoon the fish that he carried up the slope in a crude reed basket every morning, then gutted and hung them over the fire from long branches set in two opposing Y sticks. Another was a hatchet of a thin stone attached with rawhide strings to a short, sturdy branch-handle that he used to hack his way through the underbrush while foraging. The afternoons were spent in search of food, until it seemed that he had found what he could of the roots and berries, which he either ate raw or roasted over the fire in the evenings. It was then in a broken voice, that he sang songs he had learned from his loved one about the goodness around him, and he drew plans of a habitat in the dust.

Emboldened, he swatted away the flies and mosquitoes that plagued him and broke through the heavy membrane of the surrounding growth one day to stumble upon a rough trail that meandered through the thick forest of trees near the river. At that point, he became aware of others who inhabited the area. He knelt and examined their tracks mingled with those of bear, elk and deer and then followed them for as far as he dared, knowing that he was running out of his meager supplies. If he were to hunt and shoot deer, he would need powder and ammunition for his gun; he would need something to trade. Returning, he spent the greater part of his days constructing crude traps to capture the beavers, raccoons, and foxes that had dug around his camp for food scraps. He spent the following weeks tramping through the surrounding area, setting and tending those traps.

To him, the wind was a messenger, remnants of which in the late summer sighed though the leaves of the trees that rustled in reply. As each day faded into autumn, the breeze changed from gentle whispers to one which was more insistent, one which moaned as it bent branches back. No longer warm and inviting, the wind brought rain, and it became crisp with the foretaste of the icy months to come. At times it would snarl and snap and even seemed to be driving the sun away over the horizon and under darkening clouds.

2

THE OUTPOST

One morning, he scrambled awake, shivering, and rummaged about until he found and unrolled a canvas cover from around some clothing he had kept aside to wear on days such as this one. After climbing down the embankment, wading into the river and bathing in the chilly waters; he returned to don his buckskin outfit and bundle up a mound of pelts, a couple of them from red foxes, which would bring him an ample return. Tying a string of them to his belt under his jacket and shouldering his musket, he walked southward down the trail at a steady pace, in search of a trading post he had glimpsed between the trees on his canoe ride up the river.

After trudging through three or four miles of dense forest, he saw the outpost in the distance, looming over the trail, which made him wary. Was he too close to a settlement? He could only hope not as he approached the long building constructed of old, grey logs wattled and daubed together. When he entered the vast main room of the store, he was surrounded by the familiar cooking utensils, hunting gear, foodstuffs in barrels and large bags, reams of calico and woolen cloth. He took in the pungent smells of tobacco, cornmeal, coffee on the shelves, and the pine wood, crackling in the nearby round, black iron stove.

The trader was a hulking bear of a man, his silver-streaked hair tied back from a wooly, grey beard around his pursed mouth. He leaned over the counter where he entwined his stout, hairy arms in his white shirtsleeves and eyed the newcomer with mild curiosity through circular glasses perched upon his hawk nose. When he arose and picked up the string of pelts the trapper had placed on the hewn oak counter and stroked the fur with his thick hands, he was unable to conceal his admiration that shined through his deep-set eyes.

"What's your pleasure," he said in a voice like walking on gravel, and looked up with anticipation at the man who roamed the store and lay items one by one on the counter. The trapper, a tall, heavy set man with his dark mustache blending in with his dark hair which hung from under his coonskin cap, its tail hanging over his shoulder, was dressed in his best. If he had wanted to make an impression on the trader, he did. His long buckskin outfit was fringed from his hefty shoulders to his beaded spats, covering his dusty shoes, all of which were decorated with red quill work. The spats were imprinted with angular designs, beads and silver buttons. His thin, black leather belt was slung around his waist and hips, holding a black sheaf with gleaming silver beads set in bezels offsetting the hunting knife handle. The upper end of the belt held a pouch, the lower end, pelts and trap chains.

"You been here long?" The trader's sharp blue eyes met the trapper's steel grey ones. The trapper shook his head, no, and held out a rifle he had pulled down from the shelf. "Now that will cost you all your supplies here," the trader said with a grin. "But if you can bring me back a couple of these fox pelts – white or silver." He patted the pelts on the counter, "that gun is yours." The trapper nodded and returned the gun.

"You know any Indians?" the trader asked. "You must have befriended some to be wearing an outfit like that." He paused, waiting for a reply that never came. "They trade here all the time. Brought me all these clothes in exchange for sacks of flour and cornmeal. I told 'em I have no use for these things, but they said they'd buy 'em back, kinda like collateral on a loan" He walked up to a section of the store where bright, beaded and fringed buckskin clothes were stored. With his back to the trapper, he said, "Have you heard about the troubles down south?" He turned to catch the trapper's reaction.

"Troubles?" said the trapper in his low, rough edged voice. He stood his ground, unruffled.

"Yeah, and it ain't that fightin' between the states I'm talkin' about;" He paused to clear his throat. "There's been a Sioux uprising right near in the Minnesota River Valley." The trader looked at him warily. "Surely you must've heard." The trapper shook his head, no, again, and began scooping his purchases into a burlap bag the trader had provided. "The

Pony Express come by here, and the word out is it's been mighty fierce, I tell you; it's been bloody down there; them Sioux wanna wipe the settlers off this land, and they're damn near close to doin' it."

"Thanks for the warnin'," mumbled the trapper while he hefted the goods, off the counter eyeing and sizing them up before he heaved the bag of them over his shoulder.

"Don't mention it." said the trader, who resumed his place behind the counter, and watched him get ready to leave.

The trapper emerged from the trading post with his supplies, bulging in the bag over his shoulder, which included an iron cooking pot, eating utensils, a new hatchet, a shovel and a sleeping bag with a couple of blankets. He had wanted that rifle, had even lifted it up and scoped its sights, but had to put it aside for another day, maybe when he caught a silver fox. About half way down the trail, he sat on a fallen, faded old log and uncovered a slab of cheese and a loaf of bread he had purchased. He bit into the tangy cheese and an aromatic crust of bread, chewing with a feeling of satisfaction he hadn't felt for awhile. After eating about half his meal, he decided to wrap it and save the rest for the next day. With a drink of water from his canteen, he stood, repacked everything, hefted the sack onto his back, and tramped on through the crooked shadows of the tree branches and leaves overhead. Somehow this gave him a sense of security, as if he were under cover of a camouflage canvas as the evening dusk enveloped him.

When he approached his campsite, a bevy of crows flying above alerted him that something was wrong. Looking down, he saw bear scat; with a low moan, he dropped his bag, rushed into the clearing with clenched fists and cursed his luck to see that the place had been ransacked by the black bears that roamed the trail nearby. With a beating heart, he trudged around the clearing; his boots stepped on crackling refuse while he examined the damage they had done in his absence. "Dammit!" he muttered when he found that they had rummaged through and eaten the cache of food he had stored for his return. The fish were gone and so were the berries. What they hadn't eaten they had trampled. He stood back, arms akimbo and stared at the mess until he could bring himself to approach the ashes of his campfire and kindled it again. Throwing some nearby logs onto the blaze, he retrieved his supplies, sat down on a rock next to the fire and finished the bread and cheese he had saved. Darkness was falling, bruising the sky, and the lean-to needed attending, but he retrieved his sleeping gear and stretched his tired body in it near the warmth and smell of the campfire flames with his musket and knife in hand, ready for whatever lay ahead. After the long walk from the trading post, he was dead tired and fell into a deep slumber.

In the days that followed, he continued fishing, foraging and trapping, ever aware of the changes in the weather until the chill in the air, the waving skeletons of trees that had dropped thick layers of multicolored leaves on the ground signaled to him that the winter season was not far off. So he spent the greater half of his days digging part of the foundation for the cabin he knew he would not be able to erect until spring. Instead, he reconstructed a lean-to over the portion that he had dug, lining it with logs, boughs and canvas and packing it with the supplies that he had obtained from the trading post.

At the initial snowfall, he had shot and killed his first buck, carrying its tawny, young, muscular body on his back, calculating the ways in which he would use it to get through the months ahead. It had not been a fair fight, since the buck's foot was caught in one of his traps. Writhing in pain, the animal reared back and then settled its quivering body while staring at the trapper through eyes bright with fear; but death came mercifully when the animal crumbled with one shot through the heart. "So you want to live," mumbled the trapper, who knelt down at the side of the felled animal. "Don't we all," he thought as he drew out his knife to skin and dress down his quarry while the relentless snow fell. The trapper glanced up to see a myriad flurry of flakes cover the blood stains on the ground around him, flakes which he felt on his feet and his face. His guffaw bounced against the pines as he held up his hand, dabbed with white, followed by his hysterical laugh muffled by the encompassing white world.

3

SURVIVAL

By the time the blizzards began, his hut was well fortified with foodstuffs, blankets and supplies, enough to last him through the tough months ahead, he thought. Still, he would awake in the middle of the night, shivering from the cold, his fire glowing too low to be much good while it sizzled with the drippings from the snow through the boughs of the hut. He drew his heavy, woolen blankets around him, but they seemed too damp and thin, and he tried to dry them during the day, spreading them out on the lean-to, over the fire. Even his buckskin jacket seemed inadequate when the icy winds cracked like whips across his face.

Weary and wondering whether or not he could go on one morning, he stepped out during a lull in the storms to discover a large bearskin, lying next to his shelter. He looked about hoping to catch sight of whoever had dropped it there, but instead was left with the realization that though the climate of this land could be hostile, the inhabitants were not. His luck was turning, he thought, while he lifted up the pelt and used it to hunker down under during the frigid, starry nights of the months ahead.

The winter proved to be long, dreary and treacherous with the sky like a iron grey cover, and the river, a concrete-thick sheet of ice. His supply of dried, smoked fish was almost depleted, and the deer were getting scarce, for they seemed to have become acutely aware of his presence. Attempts that he had made at carving a fishing hole through the river's solid wall of ice were futile. He had thought of blasting an opening through it with his musket, but, uncertain that it would work, he decided to save what little ammunition he had left. Living on a diet of snow rabbits, he hungered for some fish, berries and bread.

One consolation occurred the clear morning he tread on the snow that crunched and squealed beneath his snowshoes to check on a trap he had set as far north as he had dared to go. His breath unfurling like smoke from his lips, he blinked against the glare of the white world around him, squinting at the silver fox held in the trap in the distance. The animal had died with excruciating pain, something the trapper tried to avoid by tending to his traps more often than he had this one. While he squatted and sprang the trap, gutted and skinned the fox, he noticed that the animal was still fresh, couldn't have been dead for more than a day. Wrapping the valuable pelt in canvas, he left the entrails for the wolves and coyotes, who plagued his hut at night when the moon was new and his fires had died down while he slept.

Forced awake, sensing their presence, he would whack at the snarling, wily creatures with the butt of his musket and restart the fire. With increasing desperation, he guarded himself and the silver fox pelt, having buried it in a box deep beneath his cache of goods only to check on it often. With it he would be able to buy better protection than he had, keenly aware as he was that this was the season of starvation — for the wolves, coyotes, foxes and for him. He found himself sleeping during the day, and sitting up awake at night, cradling his musket during his watch by the fire that he fed, not only for the comfort of its warmth, but for the light it gave him to discern the shadows in the night. As they approached him, they would crouch, bare their fangs, and spring into the blast of his weapon, splattering their blood and guts.

Though bone weary, in the daylight he would wash his heavy blankets and buckskin clothes in the river, drying them over the fire to rid them of the stench of the dead animals, whose parts he roasted and ate. Though he did not want to attract wild animals to his shelter, he was beginning to wonder if he would make it, for the rank animal smell on him reached his nostrils and hovered over his food. *It was as if he were decaying alive, he thought.* Even the bearskin he slept under no longer smelled like bear, but like the walking dead spirits around him. At times, he fervently wished he were a bear that could hibernate and escape the treachery of the winter season.

Once the wolves aroused him in the dead of night; the fire had gone out, but he could feel their hot breath spreading over him, hear them growling, prowling around his lean-to. He swung his musket around and caught one of them, who yelped and landed with a thud against the entryway. When he fired the musket he saw by its flash of light, two wolves snarling and lunging at each other, swirling on the ground in a hailstorm of dust. "Fighting over me," he muttered, when he felt the fangs of another one piercing the buckskin sleeve of his right arm. He leapt up, yelling, and slammed the butt of his musket into the jaws of the wolf, gnawing at his arm. The pack scampered out while he, himself, collapsed from hunger and fatigue.

When the dawn broke, he awoke to find a large, grey, emaciated timber wolf, lying by his side, its jaws clamped around his arm. "A six-footer," he said while he sat up and pried the wolf's fangs from his buckskin sleeve, "probably the alpha of the pack, trying to make a meal outta me. Well, you didn't make it, did ya buddy?" he said, and stood lifting and dragging the skeletal animal away from the clearing and holding him up like a trophy. "Phaw! You've no meat for me and I've none for youl" he shook his head.: "We're no good for each otherl"

Slipping and falling, rising again, he dragged the skeletal remains across the trail to the foot of a massive snow drift where he laid the wolf prone and examined him. He was a young animal, not more than two, three years, in his prime, a magnificent leader of the pack, brought down by nothing more than the wilderness that challenged them both. *Death is the great leveler, he thought* while he buried the wolf under a massive snow bank he shoved over the half-starved animal with his bare hands, all the while the icy wind moaned and whipped at his face and hands.

He returned to his lean-to with leaden steps and was almost turned back by the stench at the entryway. Making his way to the corner where lay the frozen wooden box, containing the fox and other pelts, he picked it up and what was left of his musket. "I've gotta have something better than this," he muttered, while examining the broken gun as he left and trudged onward facing waves of swirling, whining winds on the way to the trading post,

4

A SAFE HAVEN

The trapper who presented himself at the trader's was an entirely different man than the one who had first entered the post. Framed by straggles of oily hair, the trapper's face was cavernous, his eyes, deep set under a bony brow. His lower lip protruded with the effort of every step he took, and his ragged buckskin garb appeared bulky over his gaunt body. Repulsed by the smell he emitted, the trader welcomed the stranger anyway.

"What have you got there for me? I'm Trader Caldwell, by the way, but you can call me Ben," he said in his gravel voice while prying open the wooden box the trapper had placed on the counter. "Ah," he said, lifting the silver fox pelt up and into the light. Then laying it lovingly on the counter, he said, "This will make any lady's outfit look fit for a queen." Suddenly, he saw the trapper stagger. With a quickness that belied his heavy set build, the trader stepped around to the other side of the counter and was at the trapper's side, guiding him to an old wicker chair near the stove. "Take it easy now, fella, while I get you some cider."

Pulling up a chair across from the trapper, Ben looked over his cider mug and into the other man's steel grey eyes as he lifted his mug. "I don't think I ever got your name," he said.

"Jon," said the trapper in a hoarse voice, "Jonathan Griswold." He took a swig of the cider; sighed and licked his lips.

"What can I do for you, Jon?"

"You can help me replace this," said Jon, setting his broken musket on the plank-wooden floor between them.

I've got just the thing for you" Ben took a gulp of cider. "It's a brand new Baker rifle; much better at fighting off those....

"Wolves," interjected, Jonathan. "Wolves it was. They just kep' on comin' and comin'."

"How'd they get in your cabin?"

"No cabin yet." Johathan waved a skeletal hand. "Didn't have time..."

The trader gave Jonathan a long, hard look, and then finished off his mug of cider and trudged back to the counter where he clanked his mug down. "I'll tell ya what," he said peering into the large, wooden box that Jonathan had brought. "You've got fox, rabbit, otter and beaver pelts in here. That'd pay for your gun and lodging. You'd be one of many trappers who stayed here for a spell. I've got a cot in the back, and some of those Indian clothes might be useful to you until you get your own. I don't think the Indians are ever coming back for them — not after all the troubles down south of here. A bunch of 'em got hanged, I hear, and the president banned the rest. There's a bounty on everyone of 'em's head."

Jonathan looked up, interested, took a swig from his mug and leaned back, knowing that Ben was anxious to tell him everything he knew.

"There was a Sioux uprising, they call it, a regular revolt." Ben said, leaning over the counter. "They damn near burned down all of New Ulm. But they weren't able to fell Ft. Ridgely because of the rain, they say. From the reports, I was afraid the fighting would spread to here. Then President Lincoln sent reinforcements, the Fifth and Seventh Calvary with Gatlin Guns. Those Indians didn't stand a chance. Most of 'em was mowed down in a valley at Wood Lake, and the warriors who survived was hung – thirty - eight of 'em. The settlers celebrated and the government issued a ban on all them Indians here in Minnesota. They was driven out,' sent West to Indian Country. There's a bounty on the head of any Sioux caught here, did ya know that?"

Trapper Jon shook his head. "I didn't know nuthin about this here, revolt," Instead of commenting further, he looked in wonder at the new rifle Ben had brought over to him, took it and examined it, running his chapped hands up and down its stock.

"Now you wait right here while I get things ready for you," said Ben, who scurried off into the back room and returned before the sunset showed shadows through the dim windows.

He placed a bowl of soup and a saucer of bread in front of Jon, and asked, "How long did it take for you to get here?"

"Well, I had to stop and rest a few times along the way,: Jon looked at him sheepishly,"

So it took most of the day, I guess." He slurped down the hot soup and devoured the bread.

"Then you can't leave here at nightfall with it looking like another blizzard's on the way.

Here, come with me." Ben showed him the rack of Indian garments, and Jon selected the plainest ones he could find. "Here, take this buffalo coat, too. I think it belonged to the chief." Ben ushered him into the back room where there was a tub filled with hot water. A large cake of soap, a scrub brush and towels were on the stool next to it. A cot was nearby.

"And that vermin infested stuff you're wearin'. If ya put them outside the door, I'll burn 'em for ya." said Ben as he left and shut the door behind him with a guarded look at the weather-ravaged and wretched trapper.

Jon slipped out of his clothes, opened the door a crack and shoved the bundle outside it. In the chill air he walked bare-naked up to the elongated wooden tub to slide with a grateful sigh into the hot bath water. It was like a baptism, he thought, remembering when he was a young man and the preacher immersed him and a group of converts into the wide, blue Minnesota River. But that water was cold, he thought; maybe so you would be sure to rise again; he chuckled while he reached for the brush and soap. After a thoroughgoing lathering, he rinsed, stood, and stepped out to towel himself vigorously, finding the underwear the trader laid out for him to be a bit large, but comfortable. Refreshed yet worn out, he shuffled over to the cot and slipped under the quilt cover, feeling like a babe in his mother's arms, a feeling he dare not indulge in if he were to survive the days ahead.

Though he dreaded the return to his shoddy shelter, after two days of food and lodging through storms with winds that shook the trading post's doors; Griswald stood by a snow covered window as if he could tell by the faint glow of sunlight what the future would be like for him out there. With some consternation and noise, he packed up his gear and rubbed his hands against his new Indian outfit. Even the simplest, least adorned clothing that he chose from the outpost's ware looked like Indian-made buckskin. Nothing could be warmer than the fur-lined moccasins, he thought, consoling himself while wondering if a member of the Third Regiment might decide he was a Sioux who no longer had the right to live in this state. With that thought in mind, he threw on the heavy elkskin coat given him and turned to shake hands with the trader.

"You'd better get crackin' on that cabin of yours," Ben warned, while Jon grimaced.

"I'll have plenty of good days ahead for that…" Jon mumbled softly, as if he weren't sure. "There's always hope, you know."

"Better days gotta come soon. Winter's worst storms are over, I reckon" Ben shook his head and watched the tall, gaunt figure open the door and step outside in the frigid air. Though he thought the trapper was a strange, aloof man, he admired him for his courage.

Jonathan shouldered his pack of goods and trudged down the path with a travois holding bales of hay; he turned at the bend in the road to look back, not at all surprised to see Ben still standing there in the doorway of the trading post, as if he were making sure that his new customer made it. For the trader was not a sentimental man, Jon knew that. He was sizing him up and trying to decide whether or not Jon was a good business prospect. How much more could he get out of dealing with a trapper, who seemed, at this time, down on his luck? Somehow, in spite of his haggard appearance, Ben made the judgment call that Jon was a good investment. The fact that Jon wanted to leave as soon as he did showed that he was not the kind to lean on anyone; and his restlessness as he waited for the storms to pass showed that he was anxious to be on his own. The comforts of the trading post cabin meant little or nothing to him, for comfort was not what he needed. What he wanted was a place of his own and the chance to prove that he was man enough to make it against all odds in this wilderness that somehow formed you into more that what you could be anywhere else. He was a man who embraced nature as if he were courting a beautiful woman, terrifying because she was without mercy. Nothing could turn him away from that challenge.

Finally, he plodded into the clearing that he wanted to shape into something of his own, unaware that the surroundings were shaping him as well. The shadows bent and shaded the large mound of snow that looked like a half opened tomb, rather than his home. He unloaded his pack and entered the lean-to, inundated with clean, newly fallen snow, and he thrust away most of the drift inside and laid a tarp over it, then scatter the bales of hay from the trader, which formed soft, sweet smelling bedding over which he laid the bearskin where he sat at its edge to build a fire. With two Y stands and a spit to roast parts of some of the rabbits that he had shot and killed along the way back, he settled down to ride out the rest of the winter.

At first, he tried not to notice the eerie stillness that surrounded him. Not a sound, not even a bird song, nor even the rustle of a squirrel scrambling along the tree branches escaped the silence. The clearing was quiet as a graveyard; he wondered if the raging storms had killed all the living, breathing creatures that had enabled him to survive. Had his determination led him into his own death trap? As he settled down for the night, the winds seemed to answer him with deep throated moans and groans. If he had expected an end to a brutal season, his hopes were dashed. The icy winter winds struck back with a vengeance while he remained in what had become his life raft, riding out the dark, whip lashing days ahead. If it weren't for the supplies from the trader, Griswald would not have made it through that fierce Minnesota winter.

5

SPRING BLESSINGS

At last, he awoke to the steady drip of the snow melt from the tree tops. He arose and stuck his head out the entryway to watch in dazed wonder as snow receded on the ground in rivulets running toward the thawing river. As he drew back, he brushed against a pouch stuffed with cornmeal that he grabbed and pulled from the twigs wrapped around like a ghastly doorpost. How long it had been there, he did not know, but he crouched and mixed it with pools of water from the snow, forming the flour into the cakes he craved. After he searched for a pan, he structured a fire with dried twigs that he ventured out and yanked from thr lower limbs of the surrounding trees. He was massaged by the warming weather, but his dugout that he sat in was becoming muddy and most of the foodstuffs that were left were stained with mold and mildew. Having eaten his hastily cooked flapjacks, he spent a day cleaning out his living quarters while salvaging what he could for a decent meal that evening. Stoking the fire, he climbed into his sleeping bag, lay back and breathed in the fresh breezes, which were like whispered prayers that night that lulled him into a deep sleep.

At dawn, he ventured forth in an attempt to find some fresh food, and in the process stumbled upon his hidden benefactors. While shoving his way through the underbrush toward a thicket of fir trees on the hillside near the river, he spied a small band of deer. Emerging, he lifted his gun to his sight and steadied himself for his first decent meal of the season when he felt a rough hand grab his shoulder and pull him back. He whirled to look straight into the face of a full-blooded Dakota whose long, black braids were slick with oil, entwined with feathers. and whose rustic buffalo skin outfit rubbed against his own. The Indian held his other hand up to the trapper's mouth in a motion for him to be silent. The Dakota made a slight gesture with his head toward the river bank where stood a group of deer. Among them were several bucks. Two more Dakotas, similarly dressed, appeared, not far from the deer. As if given a signal, one lifted a rifle and shot it, the retort echoing through the forest, while the other pulled back on his bow and released a spinning arrow, inserted another arrow and pulled back to release it also. Their simultaneous actions let fly the bullets and arrows that felled two of the bucks while the rest of the herd reared, startled and scattered, sending the sounds of their clattering hooves thundering across their trail.

The Dakota, tall, muscular and swarthy, giving off the aroma of sweat mingled with tobacco, threw his arm around the trapper's shoulders. "Come," he said in a low voice, and then shouted to the other hunters in their Dakota language. They were laughing over each other's remarks, but the trapper understood them and knew that they were ridiculing his clumsy hunting skills. He looked down at his rifle and boots, and at their rifle, bow and arrows, and fur lined moccasins.

"Nice work" he shouted at them in Dakota, "I couldn't have done better myself."

They glared at him with a mixture of disdain and respect for a loner who survived in spite of his own shortfalls. The one with the bow and arrow was the oldest and the trapper noticed that part of his right ear was cut off over which a scar was leading down from it and around his chin.

The taller, strapping younger one with the rifle, laughed and shouted,"You show me a deer you've killed without a snare, and I'll believe you," he yelled with a look of defiance across his pock marked features.

The trapper was about to answer when the Dakota next to him, pulled him back to confront him. "You want to help?" said the Dakota whose angular eyes, high bridge nose and cheekbones were set off by his wide grin. "Then you can come and eat with us. Or we'll leave you here with nothing."

The brave let go of the trapper and walked on ahead, intent on his mission to bring back enough meat to make a good meal for the tribe. His apparent disinterest in him, left the trapper with an uneasy feeling. Knowing how far off were the chances at finding more deer anytime soon, he followed them and agreed to help. When they realized that he spoke Dakota as well as they did, their curiosity was stoked all the more. They gutted the deer on the spot, leaving the left overs for the wolves and bears, while they trussed each deer's legs onto two separate tree limbs they had cut down. Hoisting up the four stakes, they carried the two deer, hanging from the two tree poles between the four of them, having recruited the trapper to shoulder one end.

Following the trail upriver in the opposite direction from the trading post, they veered north and plodded past fallen, rotted trees and stands of birches, firs, oaks, elms and maples and over intersecting trails, some marked by rocks or sticks attached to colored rags They continued through dense brush and overgrowth until, after what seemed like an endless journey, they reached a clearing where a massive settlement of towering tipis was spread out near a lake.

"Takota Wahchinksapa," a dusky Dakota woman cried out while she jumped up from where she was sitting and appliquéing designs with quillwork on buckskin clothing. Two boys and a girl accompanied her while they closed around him, and tribal members surrounded and noisily conversed with the other hunters. While they were unfastening the deer, Takota introduced Makawee Hantaywee, his wife, and three children, Tasunke Paytah with a pockmarked face, who was a brawny, pre pubescent boy, his brother, Tokala Kohana, a few years younger, and Anpaytoo HanWi, their little sister.

"She is ten winters," said her mother, while the tawny, doe eyed child peered out from around her mother's beaded buckskin dress. They both sported dimples when they smiled.

"And her name shows how bright she is, Light from the Sun, a source of comfort and life."

The tribe was alive with vigorous activity – its women were tanning hides, cooking stews, sewing quilts and turning the fields, getting ready to plant corn, tomatoes, potatoes, squash, beans, herbs, and other crops. Some were digging swales; others were planting seeds in the mounded beds; others were filling the pathways and covering the mounds with old leaves and underbrush.

And yet, there was an undertone of anxiety expressed in the furtive glances of the men who were tending their horses, dogs, guns, bows and arrows, knives and weapons. It could be felt in the murmur of their deep voices while they worked on their snares and hunting and fishing gear. Snatches of conversation could be heard about battles with the white men along the Minnesota River Valley. "After all, it is our land. They agreed to pay us for it," The complaints arose like swells of waves from a river. "What were we supposed to do? Starve?"

Jon winced, knowing that they were referring to their latest battle with the settlers, a confrontation that he had avoided by poling from the Minnesota River into and up the Mississippi. From their comments, he realized that the settlers had broken a treaty with them in order to rob them of their land, leaving the tribe to starve through the fierce winter. *So that's what it was all about, he thought while he mulled over what he had left behind.*

When they were seated around the central fire, the tribe feasted on venison and cornbread while the tall, stocky stranger they called "Troubled Spirit" told them his Anglo name, Jon Griswald, and answered their questions. Yes, he was a mixed-blood and at one time he had a full-blooded Dakota wife, two sons and land in the Minnesota River Valley. But that was where his account ended while he looked away and continued to chew on the deer meat and munch on the cornbread. They grew silent, for they knew.

"Were you down south in the valley during our battles?" asked a two-spirit shaman, Wicasa, sitting next to the village chief, Kangee Ogaleesha. "and did you know that the great father Lincoln's army hanged 38 Dakota in Mankato this winter?" Griswald looked up and, stared into the shaman's lucid, ebony eyes. "Good thing you weren't there." Wicasa lifted a bowl of brew to his lips, his beaded bracelets shivering as they slid up his arms while the bear claw necklace dangled from his neck and over his painted chest. He licked his lips, showing his fine, white teeth. "They said it was a good day to die," he finished in a nasal tenor.

6

HONORING THE UPRISING

"Tell us, Wicasa," said one of the braves next to him. The restive circle became quiet while the braves passed around and smoked the pipe and listened to their spiritual leader.

"We were there in Mankado that day, but I with Takota Wahchinksapa hid in the forests." he indicated with a nod of his head. "Otherwise, we would have been killed. We watched them build what they called the gallows, an ugly sight. The white men drove wagon loads of pine planks to the middle of a field where they built a square platform that they hoisted higher than a tall man's height off the ground. It was like a walkway around an empty square center where they had erected a pole with ropes attached to the walkway, holding it up. A pole was raised at each corner and at the center of each section of the walkway. They nailed long planks above the walkway to the tops of the eight tall poles. On them they strung ropes with nooses at the end."

"After a few days, they were finished with their sawing and pounding and they left," interjected Takota in his low, soft baritone. "Then, at night in the moonlight, with our breath in clouds before us and the cold wind chilling us, we crept past the garrison buildings and walked around the gallows or 'thing' we called it, being careful to stay on the icy paths so we would not leave our footprints in the snow. Ten nooses hung from each side of the planks, except for one, which held only eight. That meant thirty eight braves were about to be hung. *How could they do this? I thought.* And then we noticed that the poles holding the planks up that held the hangmen's nooses were not attached to the walkway, for they had gaping square holes carved around them. We counted six ropes, each of them holding up the walkway and attached like a tipi to a single rope wrapped around the pole in the middle of the thing."

Wicasa nodded. "We looked at each other and knew that with one stroke of a hatchet, a man could cut the main rope and the walkway would fall to the ground, leaving thirty eight dead men hanging."

The listeners shuddered, and Griswald reached for the pipe, which was filling the air with the aromatic smell of tobacco.

"The next day, which was the day after their Christmas, when the sun rose, we hid among the bushes and trees," Wicasa continued, "where we could see and hear everything in the clear space, sharp as a knife with the cold. It looked like the entire U.S. army marched out in their blue coats and surrounded the thing like a square around a square. Forming another square behind them were more blue coats mounted on their horses. Behind them was a large crowd of spectators. It was like a ghostly celebration with all of them breathing out gusts of steam in the freezing air. I began to shake, not from the cold, but from the feelings I felt from the crowd who were part of this calculated, cold-blooded mass murder. I could see at a glance a gleam in their eyes that was vicious and cruel."

"It was eerie, crowded with settlers everywhere, even on the garrison rooftops, yelling and pushing each other to see the prisoners when they were marched out." Takota agreed. "Some of the doomed were very young; some, very old, too old to have killed anyone. Many had painted their faces for war. One was smoking a pipe; another, a cigar. They had white bags covering their heads, folded back up to their eyes so they could see to walk. They wore blankets and decorated their clothes with feathers and whatever they could find or was given to them by their tiospaye whose members stood near the buildings and trees, shivering, holding each other, and weeping."

"We were told," said Wicasa, "that in the prisoners' quarters old man, Tazoo, called out. 'Tell our friends that we all must walk on the same path. We go first, but many of them will follow. I will go to the tipi of Wakan Tanka and be happy when I get there; but the road is far and I am slow. It will take me a long time to reach the end. I will not be surprised if some of the young braves I leave behind will pass me on the road before I reach our final home.'"

For a few, brief moments, they paused, breathing heavily, while they pondered the words of an innocent man.

"The men were singing the death song as they walked up the steps," Wicasa, said, breaking the silence and singing the song as they sang it:

"*Wakantanka taku nitawa*

tankaya qaota;

mahpiya kin eyahnake ca,

makakin he duowanca.

Mniowanca sbeya wanke cin,

hena ovakihi.

Wakan Tanka, I'm going home. I'm going home.

I'm on the road to the spirit land.

Many and great, O God, are your works,

Maker of earth and sky;

Your hands have set the heaven with stars;

Your fingers spread the mountains and plains."

All in the circle were quiet, listening to Wicasa's nasal voice winding like the sighing wind through the air. Takota broke through the somber feelings the song had created. "The military drummer gave a tap on his drum, and when the ropes were placed around the condemned braves' necks; one of them shouted out, 'today is a good day to die!.'"

Wicasa was silent, then said, "The drummer gave another tap. Although their arms were tied back at the elbows, some of the prisoners held onto each other's hands while they chanted, 'Hi! Yi! Yi! Hi! Yi! Yi!' and it looked like their feet were moving to the death song. Then the drummer gave a third tap, and I saw the shadow of a man standing by the pole in the middle of the thing they called the gallows. He heaved a lance that sliced the main rope, and with a loud whoosh, the walkway fell and the braves were dangling there like they were still dancing. The rope broke for one of them and they had to hang him again, but you could tell that he was already dead."

"I'll never forget," said Takota with a bitter edge to his voice, "the sound of our people who let out long, loud piercing wails that swept through the skies like lonely wolf howls in the night. Over their cries, moans and sobs were the loud screeches of cheers and laughter from the crowd of white people as the walkway fell and the braves were left there, hanging."

Sitting on the other side of Chief Kangee Ogaleesha were his wife, Maka Wakanda, and his five children. One of them, a young brave, Chayton Enapay, wandered around the circle to sit next to his dear friend, Anpaytoo, who looked at him and gave him a warm smile. The Chief repeated what Chief Little Crow had once said to a meeting of the tribes with the white agent, who knew their crops had failed, "We have waited a long time. The money is ours, but we cannot get it. We have no food, but here are these stores, filled with food. We ask that you, the agent, make some arrangement by which we can get food from the stores, or else we may take our own way to keep ourselves from starving. When men are hungry they help themselves." Chief Kangee Ogaleesha's wizened eyes glanced around the circle from where he sat with a carved, hard-wooden peace pipe next to him. His lengthy war bonnet showed that he had done many good deeds and had been a formidable warrior-protector as did the scars on his face and body. His heavily beaded and quilled buckskin clothing and moccasins showcased the skills of Maka Wakanda, who sat close by with her blue, yellow and red blanket wrapped around her shoulders. It felt good to be among them, thought Griswald, even if only to listen to their stories and feel their anguish over their innocent dead men or tell them about his struggles with the wolves this past winter and his problems with the raiding bears.

The glaring sun was moving from the top of the sky sending its rays into the wet earth, lifting the scent of the thawing snows from it. As the circle broke up, the children ran behind the tipis to play hoops or stick ball and the women returned to their tasks. After Wicasa honored the pipe, the men drew closer to the chief who puffed from the pipe again, and then passed it around. Blue smoke clouded the air around the group giving them the appearance of figures in a dream. Griswald puffed on the pungent tobacco whose sparks kept the half filled bowl of the pipe aglow

Wicasa stood, lifted his thin, eagle-like face, his black hair braided with colorful strips of beaded cloth and feathers streaming down his lithe, stalwart back. He had placed a wolf hide on his back with its head and jaws protruding above his forehead. "I see here before me a man who has been through many troubles," he said, his soft, tenor voice addressing Griswald.

"You travel in darkness, not knowing where the path goes, but you keep on going because you live for the red road, and it heals you."

The chief gave a deep "Ah ho!" and the rest of the men nodded. Takota watched Griswald and saw that he was not comfortable at being singled out. Before he could speak, the chief stood, disturbing the circle like a stone thrown into it. With his heavy set body embellished in decorated buckskin, he called out in his husky baritone, "This was a good day for us. The deer came back and fed us and gave us their hides for the tipis and our clothing. We must honor them in the circle dance tonight, so they will return." Then he pointed southeast. "Hear me, that is the way toward death." He turned and pointed northwest. "But that is the way to find life."

The elm, the ash and the hickory trees swayed with the wind that moaned against the stout spruce trees, and the women and children ran toward the west where silhouettes on horseback could be seen riding through the forest. "It's the scouts," said Takota, standing next to Griswald, who by that time, was standing also and watching most of the tribe scatter with excitement and run toward the oncoming horsemen. At the same time, Griswald had indicated with a gesture at the descending sun that he had to return to his own campsite.

The chief approached, and, warmly taking Griswald's hand, joined it with Takota's and said, "You come back, someday. Maybe to stay with us?" Then turning to Takota, he placed his hand on his shoulder. "Takota here will, show you the way back."

Takota turned his brawny body and whistled. From around an imposing, white tipi, bounded a barking dog, a mixed brown and black longhaired breed, pulling a travois carrying a large bundle of supplies – venison, rice, cornmeal, and blankets. "Easy, Leaps Up," said Takota kneeling and rubbing the dog's neck and ears with his strong hands. He gestured toward the bundle. "This is for you — in case the bears raided your hut again."

Griswald eyes crinkled as he snorted, smiled and laughed bitterly. "They'd find nothing today. That herd of deer you hunted was my only chance at a meal."

"Good thing we met, then," said Takota as he clicked at Leaps Up to follow while they embarked down the trail that disappeared in the thick wilderness of trees, shrubs and scrub grass tangled with wild berries and covering fallen trees, hollowed out by beavers. The undergrowth was alive with hidden creatures, squirrels, rabbits and grouse.

7

A PLACE CALLED HOME

The lower wet branches of elderberry bushes caught at their leather leggings while Leaps Up, panted and negotiated his way behind them. Cherry tree trunks, black with the thawing run off, reached upward into branches that gave off the faint scent of buds, bursting. Birds twittered and fluttered above while a mile long flock of geese, returning from the south, squawked as they flew over the lake. The ground, breaking out of its icy covering, was breathing the promise of life through the melting snows – a breath that the breezes caught up and lifted past their faces and into the brilliant blue skies glinting through the forest. Everything seemed to be awakening, and Griswald felt glad to be alive.

"You need a horse," said Takota, encouraging Leaps Up with whistles and hand signals.

Griswald grunted under his own pack. "I need a lot of things."

Leaps Up stopped, sniffed and growled at bear scat on the trail. Takota bent down and rubbed him behind the ears, smoothed his bristling fur, and urged him on. "This is not a good time for Leaps Up to be outside the camp," he said. "The bears are leaving their winter sleep, and they are hungry."

"Eh, they don't bother me none. A big campfire, a shot from this rifle will scare 'em away. It's them wolves that give me trouble." Griswald declared while scanning the ground for any more scat. "Once I get the traps set and leave the animals' innards for the wolves and coyotes, they stay away."

After they had hiked a few miles, Takota stopped to let Leaps Up rest, dropped the weapons he carried at his side, knelt and cupped his rugged hands around some pure pools of snow, drinking the cool water while Griswald did the same. They crouched there for awhile, eating some dried berries and pemmican and sharing their food and drink with Leaps Up when Griswald looked intently at Takota, who, though tall and imposing among white men, was somewhat shorter and stouter among his own people. "Where'd you get that fancy moniker there, Takota Wahchinksapa?" the trapper asked.

Takota looked up, his black eyes like sparks in the receding sunlight. He let loose a broad grin, his sharp features, softened by his pleasant outlook. "My father named me" Wise Friend" back in,,," He stroked his chin searching to remember the days when ten winters had passed for him, and Wicasa had led him into the middle of the circle ceremony to announce his name. "Wicasa declared it then, and my father told stories of how I gave wise advice; I was a good friend to have, they said. Chief Kangee must think I'll be a Wise Friend for you, since I saved your life."

Griswald sat back, startled. "How's that?" he asked and then took stock of this tough, hardy brave, whose burnished face bore creases from the brunt of years in the sun and the wind.

"When we were stalking the deer and saw you behind the trees, we knew you would disturb them and destroy the one chance we had to kill the first deer we had tracked after a long, hard winter." He paused, deep in thought. "The other two wanted to kill you, but I said, 'Stop, see what he's wearing?'"

Griswald looked down at his long buffalo robe that Takota had grabbed, staring at its design.

"Where did you get this?" he asked while he scrutinized it. "It's the chief's!"

"Uh," Griswald grunted. "Ben Caldwell, the trader, gave it to me at his post where he says the chief left it."

Takota nodded. "When you were with him, I think Chief Kangee Ogaleesha recognized it, but I don't think he remembered where he put it that you should be wearing it." Takota chuckled. "We thought you must be a friend of the chief. Besides, if they had killed you, we would've lost both the deer and you; but because I stopped them, we got the deer and saved you, and you helped us carry our load back to our village."

"Hmmm, Takota Wahchinksapa, Wise Friend, is a fitting name for you. I'll never forget it," Griswald murmured with a sudden look of gratitude.

"What will you do when you get back?" Takota asked, while he wiped berry juice from his mouth.

"Build a cabin, fish, trap, hunt, and live."

"You can live with us, you know. I knew who you were when I first saw the way you fished. Not many white men can do it Dakota style."

"My wife showed." Griswald's voice caught and grew coarse. Abruptly, he stood up and continued down the trail, clearing his throat, his steps crunching on the crumbling snow.

"Tell me someday," said Takota, following.

When they reached Griswald's place, the sun was glowering low over the west, and Takota could stay only a little while. Unhitching the laden travois from Leaps Up, he surveyed the plot of land and Griswald's lean-to dugout, which sent out a long shadow.

"You keep this for your pelts," Takota said, indicating the travois, "I can take you to the saw mill for supplies to build your house," he offered, and Griswald nodded in agreement. "Then I will bring a horse," Takota chuckled to himself while he turned and ran swiftly back up the trail with Leaps Up by his side.

That night, after a hearty venison and wild rice meal, Griswald cleared his hut of mud and muck and laid a cleaned canvas covering over the fresh fir tree boughs he had hacked off the trees nearby. He felt the eyes of the wolves and coyotes, watching and waiting for one opportune moment while he primed his rifle and cleaned his knives and hatchet, which he kept close at hand. When he turned in, his campfire was blazing and his senses were alerted to the sounds in the night even though the half moon sent a comforting slice of light across the clearing.

8

TO BUILD A CABIN

During the spring thaw, Takota arrived driving a handsome black stallion named Sable hitched to a wagon. He also brought his oldest son, Tasunke Paytah, with him. "Here you see my son," said Takota, indicating the tall, muscular young boy sitting in back. "Strong as a horse, so we call him, Tasunke; he survived the great spotted fever, so we call him, Paytah, 'Fiery One.'"

On the way to the saw mill, they stopped at the trading post where Griswald turned in his pelts. He had caught more foxes, otters, and beavers; among them was one silver and one red fox, which he traded for a gun for Takota, the other for the Dakota clothes the trader Ben Caldwell had taken as collateral on a loan from the tribe. Caldwell objected.

"These are worthless," he said, shaking his head while loading them onto the wagon. He paid them money for the other pelts, which they would use to buy lumber and parcels of cement mixture, but as they were leaving, Ben threw a couple of bags of flour onto the wagon as well.

"You haven't heard yet, have you?" Ben shouted after them.

"We heard," Takota yelled back, and young Tasunke Paytah's laugh creased lines through the streaks of black war paint under his eyes.

They arrived at the mill near a place named St. Anthony Falls, but Takota called the area, Owahmenah (Falling Waters). Amid the sounds of the rushing waters and the waves of spray that were blown their way, Takota took Tasunke Paytah aside while Griswald stood back and listened.

"This is a sacred place," the father said, as he told the ancient story to his son. "Oanktehi, spirit of waters and evil, lives under the falling waters. And there," he pointed, "is Spirit Island, where an older woman, who lost her husband to a second wife, steered her canoe with her two children over the falls, sending them all to plunge headlong into their deaths."

Then Takota noticed signs of deterioration with competing saw mills built along both sides of the river. "The Falls used to be much bigger," he commented. He squatted to look beneath what was once a drop of massive waters. "Why the white man has dug gorges underneath, probably to bring more river water, faster to the mills." He stood up and shook his head. "They will destroy what was once a great sight of mighty falling waters."

Though Tasunke Paytah listened attentively to his father and helped load lumber onto the wagon, he wandered off into the mill while Griswald and Takota haggled with the mill keepers over the cost of their supplies, Tasunke Paytah seemed more interested in the workings of the sawmill than in the stories of his father. He watched as several logs floated into the mill while others fell into the rapids below. Beside it, the tall sawmill building had a platform which surrounded the falls on all four sides while the rushing waters beneath were turning the saws. In the tall building of the mill, through its large open porch like slats were revealed the muscular workmen who shouted their directions over the grinding whine and screech of the logs as they were being sawed. At times they could be heard calling out to "Peter," to which could be heard, "no Paytah" from the young brave. "Oh, Payton," was the reply and they returned to their work, which sent the young brave back to his father, shrugging his shoulders and shaking his head with its single feather stuck on the back of the red and yellow band around his forehead.

While the horse munched on a bale of hay, the three travelers sat on the back edge of the wagon, eating their lunch of cheese, bread and berries and looking out over the rapidly developing city of St. Anthony. "We used to come here to hunt and fish," said Takota. "Do you remember?" He looked at his son who nodded in agreement.

"But it has changed, and so fast," Tasunke Paytah remarked in his adolescent tenor, staring at the city spread out before his eyes. "There is no forest left, no deer either." His voice cracked. "How can people live here?"

Griswald pointed to his money belt and pouch full of coins. "They live off this," he said.

"Oh? You can eat that?"

The three of them laughed. "Everything used to be free for the taking. Now you've got to pay for it," said Takota. "I also don't understand why the white men want to live like that." he responded to the quizzical look in his son's eyes.

"By the way," interrupted Griswald. "What did Ben mean by 'have you heard?'"

Takota looked up from his meal. He stopped to gulp down a mouthful. "Uh, who hasn't heard about the massacre at Sand Creek, where many of our Cheyenne and Arapaho friends were murdered?"

Griswald pulled his head back in slack mouth astounishment. "I haven't heard."

"At about the same time the war over the settlers' slaves was waged," Takota continued. "troops began attacking the tribes that lived west of the Hahawakpa, despite Father Washington and his Council's agreement not to settle west of that river, the one you call the Mississippi."

He put down his food and looked at Griswald. "At dawn almost two winters after we were forced out of Minnesota, a Colonel named Chivington came with over 600 of the First Colorado Calvary and New Mexico Regiment. They raided the peacefully sleeping Cheyenne and Arapaho village near Sand Creek – those U.S. troops slaughtered almost every one – men, women, children. Then, what's worse, the army mutilated the dead and made trophies out of their body parts."

"If it weren't for those who escaped to Smokey Hill Camp, we might not have known about this horrible, cowardly massacre." Takota said.

"Yeah, I think Ben's trying to warn us that things are getting worse." said Tasunke Paytah, "There's already a bounty on our own scalps since the Dakota War"

Griswald, sat up, startled and looked around. "Then you'd best be more careful and not come around here anymore."

Takota laughed. "But they've always had a price on our heads." He surveyed the area. "We know how to live with it." The father and son exchanged knowing glances."

Griswald muttered, struck by their defiance, a point of honor between them. "Where did Wicasa get that wolf hide he wore when I was there last? I think I've seen it before," he said.

"Oh that!" Tasunka Paytah responded. "I was with some hunters who found it – not far from your place."

"Huh!" Griswald smirked. "I can tell you a story about that wolf someday."

They returned to Griswald's place with a wagon load of lumber, bags of cement mix, flour, bundles of clothing, and food. After removing the supplies, Takota Wahchinksapa and Tasunke Paytah stood together, facing the sun that was sending its rays under the trees onto the river they called, Hahawakpa, but that Griswald knew as the Mississippi. The silhouettes of the staunch, sturdy father and lanky, rangy son stood in stark contrast before the clouds which were streaming out like rods, splitting the cloud's golden orb into a multitude of colors, with purple and red, reflecting their hues through the mighty waters and a signal to father and son that it was time to return to their tribe. After the horse, Sable, had a good meal and drank from a couple of buckets, and the father and son said a few final words of farewell, they moved on up the trail, taking a half empty wagon, but leaving Griswald with a full heart.

In a matter of months, Griswald had purchased the building supplies and the three of them constructed the rustic cabin to Griswald's specifications – a cement foundation with enough space for five rooms, a kitchen, a parlor, two bedrooms and an attic, facing the river. Eventually, the small house would include a front porch as well as a storage shed, woodshed and the necessary outhouse in the back. The clearing was being turned into a spacious yard, surrounded by chokeberry and blueberry bushes and wind breaks of trees. There was room for a garden and a long, stone pathway to the trail.

"I don't see why you won't set up a tipi," said Takota one day when the three of them were laying the foundation. "Then you could pack up and leave when the white man comes." With Tasunke Paytah at his side, he looked warily at Griswald. "And they are coming. Scouts tell us people have arrived from the great waters in the East, and they're on their way here."

"Well, then with a house like this," said Griswald, "I'll blend right in."

"Did you 'blend in' when you lived along the Minnesota River Valley?"

"No, but I had a Dakota wife then, and now..." Griswald shook his head, bowed with memories. "There'll be nobody but me."

"Ah," Takota, pushed back his jet black hair, wrinkled his burnished face and spat on the ground. "You have too much white man in you." But he and his son continued to help Griswald erect the inner walls and lay the outer planks with a sort of fascination over the way the white man lived. It seemed to Takota to be too confining, limited to a square cabin and divided into rooms – just like they divided their cities into blocks, separated into streets, separating some people from others, giving more space and better land to some than to others.

Takota preferred the tall, circular tipi where the whole family could gather around the central fire in the winter where they ate and slept. The fire and they, themselves, warmed each other. He remarked on this when the house was almost completed and could not help but add more observations.

"Where are you going to sleep?" he asked.

"Back here, in the bedroom."

"But you're separating yourself from the place you call the kitchen where the fire is." Takota pushed against the wall as if it were an insurmountable barrier. "How can the fire warm you here?" He walked through the parlor and stood in the doorway to the bedroom. "I think you'll need another place for a fire back here." He shook his head over the inscrutable ways of the inefficient white man. "But then you will need two fires when you would only need one– if it weren't for that wall."

Griswald approached. "I'll figure it out," he said, "all in due time, Takota, in due time."

Eventually, they constructed a fireplace along the northside wall in the parlor. Even though Takota didn't think it would keep them warm in the adjoining bedrooms, the three of them sweated over the laying of the hearth, the stone fireplace, and its chimney. When the house was completed, they sat around the kitchen table and ate while telling stories of the old days, until the sunset signaled the need for the departure of father and son. Griswald watched their wagon disappear, swaying to and fro as they road up the trail while Sable cantered with his tail held high.

9 THE INVASION CONTINUES

Takota's news that immigrants were coming was an understatement. They swarmed into the area. Some came in carriages, but most with horses and wagons. Land was surveyed and measured into lots along the trail where trees were cut down, piled up and carted away to the lumber mills while the old pathway was widened and paved over. Griswald watched each home as it was being constructed until houses began to line the streets. Eventually, the road he lived on faced a crossroads and on the corner, across from where he lived was a much larger house with a garden and a stable in the back.

People began congregating at the crossroads. One day he was startled to discover a group of men standing on the riverbank behind his house. As he approached, he overheard, "loner" and "to himself," "eccentric." *So that's what I am, he thought, then chuckled. My own mother wouldn't recognize me.*

When he approached, the group parted, and a tall, scrawny man who seemed to be their leader said, "We were discussing the possibility of using this here area for a ferryboat to cross over to the other side, that is, until a bridge can be built somewhere nearby." He turned to Griswald. "What do you think?" Murmuring with agreement, the men, who looked like they had been field hardened from years of farm work in their native Poland, turned and looked at Jon.

Griswald didn't want any trouble and so he said he'd look into it. A few weeks later he came poling up the river on a flatbed boat, loaded with equipment. After he rounded up the men he had spoken to, they helped him set up the trolley chains that reached from one tall pole to another across the riverbanks. On his boat they constructed the the pulley that enabled it to go from one side of the river to the other, and so Griswald began a thriving business that he ran on his own.

Every penny he made, it seemed, he invested in his place. He upgraded his wood stove, bought an ice box for the kitchen and covered its floor with linoleum. He carpeted the parlor and bought heavy, dark walnut furniture for the back rooms, covering the beds in the bedrooms with mounds of large quilts. He decorated the tables in the parlor with figures of stuffed wild animals, and hung a few lithographs on the walls. Most of the time, though, he sat on a kitchen chair, next to its table and rested his wet feet near the larger warm, glowing iron wood stove.

He hadn't given much thought to the passage of time until after one harsh winter, he saw how far the settlers had penetrated into the northern forest where the trail had led upstream. What was once dense, almost impenetrable growth had become wide open lots upon which homes were being constructed. He spat on the ground and cursed himself for not keeping track of Takota Wachinksapa, and so he set off at a run up the trail, which was fast becoming a street.

10

THE LOST VILLAGE

Takota saw him, as he broke through what was left of the trees and underbrush.

"Ah, 'Troubled One,'" he called while he approached from the few tents that were left of the Dakota settlement. He led his friend to the fire inside his large tipi and asked, "Why is it we always meet when the snow melts?"

He looked at Griswald, and saw his dazed, inquiring gaze at the decimated campsite, "We're moving," said Takota. "You have heard about the Great White Father in Washington's decree that we leave, that we no longer own anything here, that we go further west to what they call Indian country, the Dakotas. I ask you, how much further west must we go before there is no more Indian land to go to? The white man will take it all."

Griswald shook his head and sat down cross legged near the fire. "I didn't know," he said and ran his hands roughly through his shaggy hair. "How stupid of me not to know."

"We're not all headed west," continued Takota, sitting down next to him. "Many of us are going north, straight up the big river, the one you call the Mississippi. There's a place there near Lake Winnipeg where some of us can stay. The Canadian government has also claimed those lands, but they keep our names for them, like Manitoba (strait of the spirit)." He grunted in disgust.

"Here too," he added, poking a stick at the fire and stirring up its embers. "They use our words, and us, as if we were their exotic toys. But we need to live on this mother earth that they want so badly. Why couldn't we have lived together the way we agreed to in the beginning?

They steal our land from us and then call us thieves when we try to get it back."

"But why are you leaving now?"

Takota paused for a moment. "I think it's because we are tired of being hunted and shot down like animals, our scalps taken for bounties. There were a few before, but soon afterwards, we found too many scalped members of our tribe lying near the lake shore, and not just men, but women and children. We cannot survive this way. The chief and most of us left winters ago, maybe what you call a year, maybe two." His voice trailed off. "We really have nowhere else to go. A Pomo came wandering into our camp last winter with stories of slavery and slaughter on the West Coast."

"But that's been going on since the 49er's invaded for gold, and before then when the Spaniards set up their missions in California," said Griswald. "I was just a boy, but I remember some refugees from the West

Coast, some Navahos at our settlement. Hell, there's been fighting forever back and forth across the plains. There's no let up either."

"For every victory we have," said Takota, "the white man comes back with an onslaught so terrible, you wish you had never been born. Even so, I thought these Minnesota woods were peaceful, until Father Lincoln's war with Little Crow and our people."

Griswald looked up at the sudden entry of a stunning young woman, dressed in beaded white bucksin, who began rummaging among the packs along the tent sides in search of something. She stirred up the smell of fur pelts and canvas. "Ah, Anpaytoo," said Takota to her. "Do you remember 'Troubled Spirit'?" With a startled glance at Griswald, she shook her head, no. Griswald stared at her, recalling the little pre teen she once was, and Takota continued,. "This is my daughter, Anpaytoo; you may remember her as a young girl four winters ago," he said to Griswald, and then motioned for her to leave. She turned obligingly and walked out of the tent.

"And she's already spoken for, by a young Dakota, Chayton Enapey (Brave Falcon), the son of Chief Kangee Ogaleesha. They've been close friends since they were small. Yes, she is beautiful," Takota continued while Griswald grunted in agreement. "When we can get her brother to quit his job at the saw mills downstream, we will all go north to join the other families who've moved to Manitoba. That will be five of us, Tasunke Paytah (Fiery Horse), Tokala Kohana (Swift Fox), Anpaytoo Wi (Radiant Light), Makawee Hantaywee (Faithful Mother), and me, Takota Wahchinskapa (Wise Friend to All)"

"Makawee Hantaywee?"

"My wife. Surely you remember her. We call her Makawee Hantaywee, the Faithful Mother. And, the second son, Tokala, received his name Kohana, lately, because he is quick, like a fox." Takota chuckled and then turned serious. "And the oldest, the one we call Tasunke Paytah, the white man will never tame him, unless with their fire water..." His voice trailed off.

Griswald was thunder struck over the changes a few years had wrought. This thriving community was now a decimated remnant of what it once was. Like a rampage of army ants, the settlers had chopped down, uprooted, laid waste the land and its inhabitants who fled the onslaught.

He listened to Takota's complaints over how much more difficult it was to hunt or fish now that the game and river and lake trout were steadily declining. Soon, every living thing would be driven from the very land beneath their feet, the land where they had built their tipis and grew their crops, while the tribe, itself, would be blown away, like dandelion seeds in the wind.

Before Griswald left, Makawee Hantaywee came forward. Her one hand clasped a brightly colored shawl around her shoulders against the brisk spring breeze while from the other hand she pressed a package of rabbit meat and rice into his hands. "For you," she said.

"If you ever need anything," Griswawld arose and said to the couple. "You know where to find me."

"Oh, you mean in the shack?" Takota said, laughing even though his clothes were tattered and his face bore the creases of maturing years. "Where we would all stay in that little front room that you call the kitchen, where the fire is?"

11

THE LOST LOVED ONES

It didn't take long. By summer's end, when the bite of the incoming autumn winds promised a harsh winter, Takota, Makawee Hantaywee, Tokala Kohana, Anpaytoo, and their little dog, Leaps Up, pulling and straining forward with a travois of supplies, appeared at Griswald's. He had just finished filling the woodshed in back and was coming around the corner to relax on the front porch when he saw them, standing shamefaced at the end of his stone walk.

"Hau! Mitakuye Oyasin! (Hello! All my relatives!)" he shouted but had to restrain himself from running to embrace them and hold them close against the long, lonely days ahead. Takota's face broke into a grin while Makawee Hantaywee lingered behind with her young son and daughter beside her. After the two men grabbed each other's shoulders and pounded each other on the back, Griswald led them down the path, plying them with questions, until he stood at the doorway of his home and surveyed the small group.

"Where's the rest of your clan?" he asked.

"Tasunke Paytah is now working at the saw mills, living in a place in the city, My sons are growing as fast as prairie grass." Takota's thin face grew taut with sadness at the thought.

"Well, come on in then," said Griswald while opening the front door into the kitchen. He pulled out the four kitchen chairs from around his table. After rummaging through his ice box, he brought out a chunk of cheese, a jar of jam, a loaf of bread, some berries and greens, that he divided up among them on the platters he had stacked on a shelf around the sink. From a jug of water, he filled a pot where he plunked a string of sausages and placed it on the stove to boil. He filled their glasses with a lemon drink he had stored in another jug in the ice box.

Tokala wouldn't sit down, but ate his pieces of bread and cheese while walking around the house. "Except for furniture, it hasn't changed much," he said. "All the other houses have furnaces, did you know that?"

Griswarld nodded. "That jam we're eating's from the daughter-in-law of my neighbor, Casmir Wojcik (pronounced Woycheck), who lives across the street. He had his house built on a cement basement with a furnace. I know because I watched 'em build it. The old man buys and shovels coal into the chute to the furnace, and it pipes heat to all the rooms through vents in the floors, heating the whole house, except the attic."

Catching Takota's inquisitive glance, Griswald grunted, saying that he had foot warmers and plenty of quilts for the bedrooms. His sleeping place would be in the parlor on the stuffed sofa. Tokala Kohana would be given a cot in the kitchen with Leaps Up. Anpaytoo could sleep in the far bedroom, Takota and Hantaywee, in the near one. What more could they ask for? At least they would be safe from the marauding white men who would drive them out of what was left of their village with nothing but the clothes on their backs.

"I thought you owned a horse," said Griswald looking at them, startled at not seeing the magnificent stallion, Sable, meant to be a wedding present for Anpaytoo when she became old enough to marry Chayton.

"Sable belonged to Chayton Enapay's family, who took him to Manitoba with them. We will move up there as soon as we get Tasunke Paytah to come with us," said Takota with anxious eyes. His hope would turn into anticipation which would be reduced into deep longing, for instead of leaving soon they withstood many severe winters together. Meanwhile, Tokala Kohana grew tall and strong, taking on the stocky build and sturdy features of his father, Takota Wachinskapa. As the days grew long and when the river ice receded, they learned how to help Griswald work the ferry, with their powerful arms and strong hands gripping the chains that stretched from one end of the river to the other, while they pulled the flatbed boat that carried horses, settlers and supplies to the far side. Griswald remarked on Tokala Kohana's quick wit and supple strength, to which the young brave responded with a wide grin. Takota looked upon his second son with the pride he once reserved for Paytah, "The Fiery One," and he referred more and more to Tokala (the Fox) as Kohana, "The Swift

One." As they hunted and fished together, they replenished what they caught with the supplies Griswald purchased with the ferry money.

Anpaytoo, who also grew tall with the grace of a supple willow tree and who ran errands for Casmir Wojcik, the neighbor who lived across the street, was as unaware of her striking beauty as she was well versed in her mother's skills. Together, they dug out and prepared the land and cultivated the garden at Griswald's place, planting the traditional three sisters Hantaywee had learned from her grandparents who had learned it from the Iroquois when they had traded long ago along the Great Lakes. Squash, corn and pole beans grew together as did beets with lettuce and onions, catnip, garlic and mint or tomatoes, potatoes and cabbage. Their crops varied with the weather and the seasons, sometimes filling their small kitchen with their aromas, at other times, wilting from either too much or too little rain or pests that even a bevy of birds couldn't control. The two women grew stronger as they wrestled with overgrowth and turned under hard, resistant soil to plant and nurture the seeds of life.

The small family's hopes were high with Paytah's promise to leave with them after his next payday, that is, until Griswald failed to return from a trip to the trading post. There had been talk within the community along the trail and some hostile glances sent their way, but Griswald thought that the busybodies' lives were too small and petty to do him much harm. He had grown confident and secure in his holdings, enough to take on credit at the trading post, using his full name, Jonathan Griswald, instead of Trapper Jon.

After a sullen wait for a few more days that stretched on into a week, Takota rubbed Leaps Up's nose in Griswald's underwear and sent his son and the dog out on a mission — to find the old trapper. Tokala Kohana, led by Leaps Up, found "Troubled Spirit" sprawled out on the riverbank about two miles downstream. He had been shot, execution style, and scalped, his hands tied behind him. The bounty hunter had stuck a **WANTED** poster with a knife in his back, which Tokala Kohana knelt down to examine. Griswald's face, drawn in black and white, glared back at him. The young brave, his heart beating with fear, and his dog raced up the trail to find Takota.

12

"TROUBLED SPIRIT'S" RESTING PLACE

"We must move quickly," said Takota, who had finished ferrying a customer across the river. He put up a "closed" sign on the ferry and hitched Leaps Up to a large travois that they had used when deer hunting. As he gathered his son, daughter and wife around, he cautioned,

"We cannot act in the traditional manner, yet. We must keep quiet and cover our tracks."

And so, the native family of "Troubled Spirit" wrapped his body in a clean woolen red blanket and placed him with a bundle full of his things on the large travois that Leaps Up pulled along the trail with them. Anpaytoo and Tokala Kohana were instructed to rub out their tracks and the ruts made by the travois, using tree branches to brush away the final traces. Hantaywee carried Griswald's thick strands of grey hair in a pouch which they honored as sacred over the smoke from a sage fire before they left.

At midday they arrived at the clearing marked off by a stand of two birch trees where the Dakota settlement had once stood, but was now the vast, empty space that they crossed as they headed toward the far wooded area of their sacred burial grounds. The scaffolds creaked and moaned with the wind, their skeletal remains and ragged remnants of clothing and blankets fluttering overhead in the breeze. The sun cast jagged shadows across the sparse forest; the ravens flitted among the trees, joining their cries with the twittering of sparrows and wrens. The family sensed that the trees were filled with the spirits of the dead, who seemed to be saying, *We will dwell here, close to the sky and Giver of life, and we will never leave you.*

"Who goes there?" A shrill, disembodied cry shattered the stillness.

The party froze for a moment, and then turned in the direction of the voice. Emerging from the forest was a figure, dressed in warrior regalia. His face was painted half black, half red, his buffalo robe hung askew revealing his painted chest and buckskin leggings. The horns of his buffalo headdress cast a long shadow, and his feathered tomahawk was in one hand, a rifle in the other and bow and arrows were belted at his side.

Takota's squinting eyes opened with recognition; he dropped the tavois poles and rushed to embrace him. "Wicasa! Why are you here?" he cried out in a hoarse voice while he held the thin medicine man's shoulders and searched Wicasa's eyes.

The figure relaxed, grasped Takota's shoulders and looked into his face. "I see that you've been growing older while living with the white man," he said with an eerie smile. "I am, too, protecting what was left of us here in our sacred burial grounds." With his arm over Takota's shoulders, he walked with him over to the travois. "And what have we here?"

"Troubled Spirit," murmured Hantaywee who was standing near the deceased trapper as if she were his keeper meant to shield him from the rough winds of the nether world with her wind-blown skirts.

"Ah, the bounty hunters finally caught up with him." said Wicasa. Takota looked up at him in surprise. "The Troubled One's story," said Wicasa. "Our scouts from the Minnesota River Valley told us. I knew it was only a matter of time." He looked into Takota's eyes and motioned with his head toward the family. "You must tell them."

Hantaywee, clutched her shawl and said softly, "May we honor him in the Red Way?".

Wicasa nodded, threw his head back and cried out to Wakan Tanka while taking in the brilliance of the skies above before he looked at her, standing there, startled. "The settlers will not bother us here. I have frightened them away when they come with their surveyors and equipment. They think this place is haunted, filled with dangerous devil spirits seeking revenge."

They set to work, hacking down the saplings and branches for the scaffold which took the greater part of the afternoon to construct. After that, the commemoration began, the dance in time with the drum Wicasa beat while they wailed with high tremolos. Anpaytoo's bucksin dress swayed with the rhythms of the dance while she noticed that her father Takota's voice was trembling almost to a sob and that tears watered his eyes. At sunset, they installed the man Jonathan Griswald, known to them as "Troubled Spirit," high upon the scaffold, arranged his items of comfort around him, and continued their circle dance, after which Wicasa led them to his oaken lodge, nestled next to an elm tree at the other end of the woods.

Together they sat around the central fire outside his place while they ate the traditional feast of wild turnip, buffalo, tripe, dried meat with plates of choke cherries, wild plums, and buffalo berries. Afterwards, they made a gift of Troubled Spirit's things and his sacred bundle to Wicasa, which he embellished with eagle feathers.

"I will keep these things forever in a safe place," he said while waving them over sacred smoke from a small, separate fire filled with sage. "I will honor them while the brave warrior, 'Troubled Spirit', travels on the starry road to the good place Wakan Tanka will provide for him."

Then Wicasa stood up and cried out, "Hear me, 'Troubled Spirit', may you be troubled no longer; may you find happiness when you meet again with those who went before you." He then led them through the chanting of the death song that the thirty-eight braves had sung on the scaffold, and the group stepped a slow circle dance to his hand held drum until they were weary. "You may wonder, my friends, why we honor this particular song. It is because 'Troubled Spirit' was executed in much the same way as the others — without being allowed to tell his side of the story, without being allowed to let his family live on the land that they would die for. There is a life spirit inside us which fights to stay alive, and that is what the thirty-eight warriors were doing, 'Troubled Spirit's along with them. He was part of that battle which continues to this day and beyond, even when we are defeated through trickery and deceit."

"Ah Ho!" the family shouted in unison and cried out their fairwells, embracing Wicasa.

At nightfall, the family raced, breathless, down the pathway and past the fast depleting forests to Griswald's where Takota removed the "closed" sign from the ferry before the dawn broke through the sheltering skies.

PART TWO

13

THE SHADOW SPIRITS (1867 TO 1876)

A young woman, seated at her desk, arched her back and stretched, running her slender fingers through her long dark hair, moving her head around in a semi-circular motion, and rolling her aching shoulders. She had pieced together this account, found in the personal belongings of her great uncle, Stanley. From the leather bound, 19th century journal laid out on her desk, she was typing a copy of his memoirs into her word processor, bending over sometimes with a magnifying glass to read the faded script and add a word or two here or there for the sake of clarity. An historian, her great uncle had aspired to document the past, and, no doubt, his writings recorded his mother's and his uncle's recollections. What was left was to find the ferry house, itself, and to explore the old neighborhood.

The deluge poured down until the river was swollen, while the rain drenched the sides of the cabin on the evening after the small band returned from their funerary task. The inhabitants closed the doors tight and shuttered the windows while Takota filled the stove with more wood and stoked it into a blazing fire. They gathered around it, shivering in the gloom. Hantaywee brought blankets to cover them, and the silence filled the room with one thought only. How would they survive?

"Did you feel it?" Anpaytoo whispered clutching at Hantaywee's shawl as she sat next to her. Her mother nodded, for she had felt it too.

"It's a spirit," she murmured under her breath. "A spirit wandered in here. I felt it like a shadow, moving past us." She looked around. "It's gone now."

The shadow of the woman had moved across the room after it had arisen from the sunrays gleaming over the river, and took shape there on the shore. The cool waters had lapped at her sun-bronzed legs where she stood with her arms akimbo, looking up at the solid bluff, encrusted with rocks and underbrush. She was filled with the sensation of déjà vu.

In her jeans and beige t-shirt, her thin, lithe figure moved with a steady grace up the side of the bluff, her sandals digging into the dirt and stones. She grasped the brush and pulled herself up the steep incline until she clambered over the top. From there, she saw the small cabin and its outhouse that had to be used in the sub zero Minnesota winters. A gust of wind tossed strands of her dark, brown hair over her face, which she brushed back, her deep brown eyes squinting under her expressive eyebrows while the clouds thundered across the sky. She pursed her lips at the thought of a downpour.

But she felt an intense kinship with this place. The ancient, hewn wooden house with an attic, a home that held together three rooms and a kitchen, heated by a cast iron stove and a fireplace, must have been considered an improvement over the log cabins that had preceded it, she thought. She walked around the place, surrounded by large leaved rhubarb plants, crossed the porch and entered the kitchen where the stove had once stood. In the winter the room would have been smoke-filled with the burning of split logs from the pile out back. She walked on through the other three rooms, cold and empty and being made ready for antique furniture.

From feeling a ghostly presence, a chill seeped through her; she shuddered and wondered where she could find traces of her great grandmother, Anya. Who was she? What did she look like? Her name had been scrawled across a few documents — the local church's marriage list, her grandfather's birth certificate. Pondering her investigation, she returned and walked around the cabin to the front and onto the porch.

She pulled out an old sepia photo of her grandmother, Amelia, leaning against the front porch post near the steps. Then she strode down the steps and walked a few feet away, where she turned, stepped back, and compared the house to its faded image in the picture. Lightning flashed across the menacing clouds, casting an eerie glow over the home that had held four generations. Now it would stand open and ready for others to walk the grounds and wonder about its former inhabitants. What a wellspring of energy, she thought. Caught up in the rainstorm, which gave warning with a sudden crash, she turned and ran down the stone pathway to the street where her dampened clothes stuck to her when she slipped into her car, turning on its windshield's rhythmic wipers that swept away the dense splatter of rain while she drove on.

The moon had covered the sun that evening, and mother earth was in distress. Rushing across the street from Casmir's in the misty dusk, strafed with black clouds and lightning bolts, Anpaytoo felt the rain pelt her face and grapple with her skin through her calico dress. Slipping on the stone pathway, her shoes scrunched into puddles while she dashed with all of her supple strength through what seemed like buckets of tossed water. She called out, and through the opening door, she could see the wood stove burning and Tokala Kohana, smiling. By the time she reached the entryway, her clothes were drenched, her shoes leaked, and her hair hung like limp, ripped, black rags around her face.

Having crossed into the back bedroom, she changed into a faded white cotton nightgown, covered herself with a blue, yellow and green striped blanket, and returned, her bare feet padding across the floor to where she sat at the table while the family shared a pot of hot, thick venison stew. After the meal, mother and daughter whispered about the darkness of the day, which allowed a spirit to pass through. Anpayto's heart was racing, but the family was consoled by the candle in its long wooden holder, its light dancing off their faces, burnished by the glow highlighting the high cheekbones of Takota Wachinskapa's swarthy face as he leaned back in his chair, making his pipe ready for the tale he was about to tell. He had a knack for storytelling, and Griswald's was one he would never forget. After a few puffs on his pipe that filled the room sith a pungent aroma, he said, "First know this. He had a wife, a full-blood Dakota; Ehawee (Laughing Maiden) was her name; and two sons. Ciqala (Little One), and Wanahton (Charger)." Takota said. "He told it to me in this way:"

14

JONATHAN GRISWALD'S STORY

"Well, son? What did you learn from the council meeting?" Jon Griswald's low, gruff whisper emerged from the dark recesses of his trading post.

The boy turned in the gloom of the evening; the hatchets, arrows and muskets, that hung on the walls, gleamed in the shafts of the rising moon. He stood still. Soon he felt the buckskin clad arms of his father around him. Kneeling next to him, the trader awaited the boy's news from the council meeting.

"They want war," he whispered, his large, dark eyes staring directly into his father's pair of steely grey ones.

"War?" His father pulled back a little. "So this was a War Council?"

"I don't know. The braves shouted back and forth. The chief wouldn't agree with them. Then he made a speech, something about dying with them. And then the braves left."

"Little Crow didn't want war."

"He said they were sure to lose, that there were too many white men; they would keep coming and coming and couldn't be stopped." The father held the boy close and slipped a piece of molasses candy into his son's hand.

He stood up and shook his head. "That's not good, not good at all."

"Why don't you talk to them? to Chief Little Crow?"

Griswald patted the boy's head, tousling the jet black hair. "Me? I'm a part Indian man who runs a trading post built by white men. The Dakota won't listen to me."

"Am I part Indian, too?" The boy's small breeches were torn and hung loose around his knees. His shirt was soiled and ready for the wash. His black hair framed his face and hung down to his shoulders.

"Considering your mother's full-blooded Dakota, I'd say yes, but you have more Dakota in you than I do." Griswald took the boy's arms. "C'mon, let's go home to your mother and little brother." He hoisted the eight-year-old upon his shoulders.

"Does that mean if I marry a full-blooded Dakota, that my kids will have more Dakota in them than me?" The boy's high pitched voice trailed off while his father locked the bolt to the post and trudged on towards the cabin behind it. "I guess so, I guess so"

"Then if those kids marry a full blooded, will their kids have more Dakota blood?" Griswald, nodded, yes.

"When would the Dakota blood take over?" he piped in his high voice.

Griswald threw his head back and with a deep guffaw, laughed so hard that he almost bounced his son off his shaking shoulders. "Whenever you want it to, son."

Pushing open the door to their cabin, shafts of light from the fireplace spilled out onto the walkway. Ehawee was bending over the kettle, stirring the evening meal that she had made out of what she had harvested from their garden. She looked up, her cat-like eyes flashing in the firelight while one of her black braids slipped over her shoulder. "How did you do that? How did you turn your father into your pony?" Wanahton (Charger) laughed and jumped down, running over to smell the aroma from the cooking pot. His mother stood up, her buckskin dress stretched like a swag around her; she was plainly pregnant. "Shhh, Ciqala (The Little One) is asleep already." She whispered while she motioned toward the small cot near the fireplace. "He plays hard, and was angry that Wanahton went to the council without him."

"They would've distracted each other," said Griswald softly while opening a pack he had tied to his belt, and pulling out a freshly killed rabbit. "This'll add some flavor to our stew."

Ehawee deftly took it, skinned and dressed it, cutting the meat into small pieces that she added to the pot. "So what did Wanahton find out?" she mumured, bending over the meal.

The child's voice rang out like a bell. "They're going to war. "Tosta nici matekte!"

"Hush," said Griswald. "Keep it down."

"Tosta nici matekte?" Ehawee echoed while she looked up.

"What? Where did you hear that?" Griswald grabbed Wanahton by the shoulders and knelt down to gain eye contact.

"The chief. He said it."

"Taoyateduta?" Ehawee whispered the chief's name and stood with both hands held over her heart.

"The chief's a brave man to say he'll die with his warriors, but that don't meant it's gonna happen." Griswald looked up at his stricken wife. "We'll talk about this later."

So she filled the bowls and they sat around the table, eating until they were filled with the hot meal. Griswald broke through the silence with the tale of his adventurous hunt for the rabbit.

"If that rabbit hadn't jumped out from behind the woodshed, I woulda sworn he was a ghost rabbit, his tracks disappearing like they did," Griswald chortled. "As it was, he scared the livin' daylights 'otta me. If I warn't so hungry, I mighta missed him, but I got him anyway." Ehawee's and their son's laughter almost awakened Ciqala, who moved and then settled back with a satisfied, cat-like smile. Once he had eaten, Wanahton was tired and ready to wash up and slip under the blankets of the cot next to his brother. Ehawee and Griswald worked in unison, sweeping and cleaning their cottage. He gripped the brass shovel and broom and swept up the ashes from around the hearth where he covered the andirons with fresh logs over the embers. With some starter sticks and the bellows he forced the logs to succumb to the heat long enough to burst into flames.

All the while, Ehawee scrubbed down the kettles and dishes in a round tub filled with warm, soapy water. When done, she wiped her hands on her skirt and felt the growing infant in her womb move. "Oh! Our baby is alive!" she exclaimed.

"Yes, Indeed!" He added as he came from behind to embrace her and hold her swelling body. They were a handsome couple, something they appreciated as they slipped into bed. In the dark recesses of the cabin where the moonlight flickered as he stroked her tawny skin while her upturned face broke into a smile.

"How lucky I am to have you," he murmured. "You're so beautiful."

"And I, you," she responded, caressing his muscular arms and embracing him as well as a pregnant woman could. "Oh!" She pulled back. "Someone is trying to kick through." She placed his hand on her womb so he could feel the movement. He let it slide around her body to give her a long, lingering kiss. After awhile when they were resting together in their embrace, Ehawee's eyes lit up like sparks in the dark, and she whispered, "What does this mean? This council of braves, have they gone mad?"

"I hope not. God Almighty, I hope not." They drifted off, holding each other close.

When they awoke in the morning light, he leaned on his elbow beside her. "One thing it does mean," he said, "is that we must leave."

"Many are moving West," she murmured

"Let's go North – up the Mississippi. There are some Dakotas in Canada."

"But out West, there's buffalo."

"Phaw!" He snorted while throwing the blankets back and sitting on the edge of the bed. "By the time we arrive there, the white man will have done to the buffalo what they did to the deer here."

"She sat up, nodded in agreement and looked sadly at his angry face. "They're like a whirling windstorm, destroying everything in its path."

"But they'll leave us alone up North, and I hear that the fish in Rainy River and the game are still plentiful."

"But that's Ojibwe territory."

"We'll go past them, further north."

"Where are you taking me? To the home of our ancestors?" She cried out, and Ciqala and Wanahton stirred. Without saying another word, the couple arose, dressed and started to pack for the trip.

Griswald opened the Trading Post as usual, but stashed away supplies in duffel bags. Natives wandered in and out, eyeing the weapons. An old native, leaned against the counter and grinned, ready to talk business, but walked away when he saw that Griswald was too distracted with other things on his mind. Griswald approached him at the door, but the old native, only looked at him, turned and walked away while singing a plaintive death song.

Everyone knew that the Dakota and Lakota crops on the strip of land they now occupied had failed, that the game was ravaged because vast tracts of land were cleared and plowed by the white men. They all knew that President Lincoln in Washington was too busy fighting a Civil War to honor his treaty with them, to honor the annuity payments for the land the settlers were now occupying. Traders wanted the money first, claiming that the Indians "owed it to them." The Dakota and Lakota wanted it, themselves, as due them in payment for their land, but the gold bullion never came.

As the days stretched on and Griswald's wagon was almost ready, he had hoped that Little Crow would be able to negotiate something at the next meeting with the trader. But instead, word came back that the agent, Andrew Jackson Myrick, told the Dakota, as if they were animals, to "eat grass or their own dung" Their world, once rich with forested life, had been stripped bare, while the white settlers used the land they had claimed and farmed to fill their graineries with excess they would rather see go to waste than share it with "redskins."

As late summer swept in with falling leaves and cold winds, Griswald was determined to secure the wagon with plenty of supplies tied down and packed into its corners. One day, after he saw to it that their old mule, Molly, had enough hay in her shed, he decided to go on another trip to track down more game. It was a futile effort, he realized after trudging through the barren forest, its denuded trees swaying with the wind's moans. Even though his approach was stealthy, nothing appeared, not even a rabbit. Finally, he spied a few wood grouse and shot them down. Returning with the game in a bundle at his side, he saw from afar the doors to the Trading Post wide open and swinging in the wind, banging against the building, something Ewahee, who often ran the trading post, would never allow.

"Ewahee and the boys!" The thought struck like a lightning bolt through his heart, already heavy with foreboding; his mouth felt dry. He dropped his bags of prey and forced his tired legs to race toward the post. Bursting through the entryway, he saw that the hatchets and muskets were gone, as well as blankets, knives and other supplies that warriors would want. Strangely, everything else was untouched and left in order. It was quiet, too quiet.

"No!" he whispered and then yelled, "No!" Through the store, out the back door and down the pathway he raced and burst into the cabin where he saw a soldier scalping Ehawee while he straddled her mutilated body, lying in a pool of blood oozing across the floor.

With a primal scream, Griswald swiftly grasped his hunting knife from his holster and threw it at the startled soldier who turned in time to receive the blade that plunged between his eyes and into his skull. When another soldier entered, Griswald leapt behind him, and, ranting with rage, twisted his head with a ferocity that broke his neck, killing him instantly. "Kill me," Griswald wailed, "Kill me too." Slowly, he knelt, shaking with sobs, waiting for the inevitable retaliation until he realized that he had burst into the middle of the dirty work of local militia scouts.

In the silence of the room, he stopped, looked around and from their uniforms, he figured that the two were sent ahead by the U.S. brigade that would soon follow. He crawled over to Ehawee's body, where, racked with his gutteral moans, he wept over her and the severed fetus next to her, a nascent little girl. He lifted the tiny blue infant and with trembling hands laid it in Ehawee's blood stained arms, taking her hands, which were extended outward in resistance, and folding them around it. "Takchawee Weeko," (Pretty Dove) he named her between sobs. Then he stood, trudged to the corner where he grabbed three of their brightest blankets. One, he wrapped around his wife and babe, and the other two, around each son. As he bent over them, he moaned in agony at the sight of his two boys, shot and killed, He lifted them to his heart and took one last look at their faces. Wanahton's eyes were as open and trusting in death as they were in life; Ciqala's, closed as if he, mercifully, never saw a thing.

Throughout the blood splattered cabin Griswald stumbled while he kicked and shoved aside the military scouts' bodies as he carried his precious cargo away. He loaded them onto the wagon, hitched up their old family mule, Molly, and drove to the outskirts of New Ulm in the twilight where he dug three graves, lowering them, one by one in the fetid smelling loamy soil, placing their favorite objects with them. When it came time to cover them, though, he trembled so much that he could not lift the spade. Instead, he slowly collapsed into sitting there cross legged throughout the night and wept in a lonely vigil of hope against despair. The night owls swept past him, screeching over their prey; wolves howled and coyotes barked in the distance.

As the dawn revealed his family's forlorn, misshapen forms, he managed to stand and shovel the earth over them, returning them to their primeval womb. For awhile he hesitated before covering Ehawee; the thought that he would never lie with her again was more than he could bear. He wanted to climb into the grave with her, and claw it down upon them, but from her little bundle under the blanket, one hand had pointed upward in the dark, and she seemed to be urging him to finish the job and go on. After covering them with mounds of earth, he placed stones around them, grateful that he had the chance to spare their bodies from any further desecration.

With a sad, slow pace, he climbed aboard the wagon, and drove the mule along the route that he and Ehawee had chosen. When he reached the town of Henderson, though, his plans had changed; he traded Molly and the wagon for more supplies and a canoe that he paddled up the Minnesota River until it forked into the Mississippi while it was turning icy with the approach of the oncoming winter.

"So that is Troubled Spirit's story," said Takota Wachinskapa. Sparks cracked against the dying embers in the old wood stove where the family was seated with the dog, Leaps Up, sprawled at their feet.

"We must leave this place," Tokala Kohana's low voice pushed through the silence Hantaywee drew closer to Anpaytoo, adjusting the blankets around them. They both shivered in the cold, still darkness, Hantawee regarded her daughter with nerve wracking anguish.

"We will talk about that in the morning," muttered Takota, bending down to pat Leaps Up, who lifted his tawny head in response.

"You knew about this? All this time? Did you not know how dangerous this was for us?" Hantaywee's voice was quivering with rage. "Did you not know that we are living in a time of great warfare – unlike any that we have ever seen before?"

"When have we not been at war?" Takota retorted.

"Phah! Those were like friendly skirmishes between rivals compared to the white man who comes like a mighty, wailing wind uprooting everything in its path."

Takota's head nodded, barely perceptible in the evening shadows. He continued with a cerain glum assurance. "As long as no one knew about it, we were safe. Troubled Spirit gave us some protection. And the people here still don't know."

"Oh, well then, how long are we going to wait for them to find out?" Hantaywee stood, gathered up her blanket, and motioned for Anpaytoo to follow.

15

THE EXILES

Streams of daylight filled the front bedroom, spilled over the bed piled with blankets and quilts and glinted on the faces of Anpayto and her mother where they lay with their heads on plump white pillows and their lithe bodies wrapped in bedclothes under a mound of covers. Both were awake and lying there, resting in the few warm moments before one of them would be the first to slip out of bed and head for the outhouse in the brisk springtime air.

"Are you there?" Hantaywee whispered. "You are so still that you seem to be somewhere else."

"I am, here and yet not here. Awake and yet not awake, for I am remembering Chayton."

Hantaywee turned to look at her daughter's radiant face, upturned and staring as if she were in another world. Chayton Enapay had chosen Anpaytoo the first time that he saw her when they were both very little.

"We used to play alongside the river, wading in it, pretending to spear the fish, laughing at the minnows darting in and out. The water was so clear. Then we'd play stickball and sometimes I would win and he would make funny faces at me, and then, just before he left, we would meet at a sacred place in the woods where he told me he would never forget me; that we would be together someday."

"Yes, I remember, my daughter. You two were so noisy with your games, until before Chayton Enapay left when you showed up, dressed in your finest regalia, looking so pretty in the white doeskin, fringed dress that I had appliquéd with a sun burst of beads around the neck. And your braids were intertwined with more beads and feathers as well. He couldn't stop looking at you, even though you were still too young to leave with him, but he promised you Sable,"

"Does that mean that I am promised to him?" Anpaytoo sat up and turned toward her soft spoken mother.

"Yes," her mother whispered.

"How were you promised to my father?" she asked in a timid voice, barely heard.

"It was different for us," Hantaywee said, sitting up and leaning back on the elbows of her tawny, muscular arms, her black hair tousled around her sculptured, brown face. "Takota came from the East with a tribe that was forced to migrate west. We were already here when they joined us and I was already of age. So we invited him to our tipi and I served him a meal."

"Oh," Anpaytoo pulled her knees up and hugged them. "Was that it?"

"Not really, for we were both with our families who asked a lot of questions."

Hantaywee smiled and turned to her daughter. "Every couple gets to know each other in different ways. Ours was a much quieter way than yours."

"But I would like to serve Chayton Enapay a meal…" Anpaytoo bent over and whispered in her mother's ear, "Quietly."

"Maybe someday you will." Hantaywee smiled, looked up, yawned and stretched her arms out.

"Mother," Anpaytoo sat up, turned and reached over to grasp Hantaywee's thin. sinewy shoulders and looked intently into her her eyes. "Let us go now. Let us leave this place where a killer comes out of nowhere to murder our friend and where a spirit brushes against us like a bad omen."

Hantaywee sat up straight and took Anpaytoo's slender hands in her rough ones. "You know we cannot leave without Tasunke Paytah. We cannot abandon him."

Anpaytoo moved away in pain, and jumped out of bed onto the ice cold floor. "That means never," she moaned.

"No, Takota will find him and bring him with us."

"He has already found him and only comes back with the white man's coins."

"That was before."

"Before?"

"Our friend was killed." Hantaywee pushed back the covers and sat upon the side of the bed. "We will have to talk about our plans tonight when we all meet. Your father, Takota, will explain."

Anpaytoo quickly dressed, gathering her red and yellow shawl around her, and headed out back. Once there, she walked across the clearing, clambered down the river bluff and onto the shore, letting the brisk spring morning breeze caress her exotic features and the cold waters lap over her bare feet. While chanting an ancient song that lilted across the river, she turned toward the east where the sun shone on her face, and she spied the morning star and sang out with a lilting voice, "Oh Wakan Tanka, thank you for the sunlight sending life beating in me and all living things." While the breeze lifted her hair around her devoted presence, she noticed an eagle perched on the oak tree upstream and watched it plunge past her while it scooped up a river trout. Under its powerful wings which cast a shadow over her as it soared upward and toward its nest, she continued,"May the Eagle Spirit guide me to follow the red road that lies before me." Turning to the south where the sun shines, she sang the song Hantawee taught her, "Oh Mother Earth, nourish me and all who walk upon you, fly over you and grow from you." She recalled the wolf howls she heard in the night and prayed: "May the Wolf Spirit help me to remember my relatives – two legged, four legged, or winged, all creatures and plants, and help me follow the path ahead and love all that lives." Shifting toward the west where she had seen the sun set and thunderheads rise, she intoned, "Oh Spirit where life meets death, awaken us; like the hibernating BrownBear, heal me and all my loved ones, so that we may be at one with all creation." Finally, she turned toward the north where she believed life is made new, and pleaded, "Oh my ancestors who are always with me, call on our White Buffalo Spirit to help me wisely accept change and guide me into the spirit world." At that moment, she felt in harmony with every living thing and time and space seemed to meet in the prism of herself.

She spied a human shadow with a dog on the other side of the river and, startled, clambered up over the river embankment, feeling the rough rocks and earth under her bare feet. She ran past the familiar outhouse, then past the woodshed, to and around the cabin, up the three front steps and into the kitchen where Hantaywee, Takota and Tokala Kohana were standing at the stove while Hantaywee was tending the flapjacks. The smell of coffee, fresh, toasted bread, honey, butter and oatmeal filled the room. Leaps Up was curled under the table, eying the group, waiting patiently for crumbs.

"Let's eat!" Tokala Kohana shouted, his black hair swaying around his strong, young features and over his shoulders while he grabbed a chair with his rough hands, followed by the others with chairs scraping the floor while seating themselves around the table. Griswald's chair stood empty, backed up against the far wall. Each glanced at it and then resumed eating in silence.

Takota looked at them with wizened eyes as they stared down at their plates while they munched on their food. "He was gone so often, you would think that he had not returned yet," he said in his gruff voice.

"I know," said Tokala Kohana. "But he's not coming back this time. What does that mean for us?"

Hantaywee reached out and placed her hand on his shoulder. "We'll talk about that later, son. But for now, you and Takota need to get things ready. People might come to use the ferry."

"And I have to go help old man Casmir," Anya murmured, looking out the window, adding. "I have to be on time."

"On time?" Tokala Kohana asked, his young voice changing from a youth's to a young man's tenor.

"The old man told me one day that I was not on time, that I was late. Then on another day, he said I was too early. And so I noticed that when I was on time, the shadow from the house was a certain length when I left, like it is now." She stood up. "So I'd better go." She bent to pull on and tie her shoes that she had left at the doorway and clutched the shawl around her shoulders as she pushed the creaking screen door open and gently let it slam as she stepped outside. The family watched her walk down the stone pathway until her slender form disappeared around the bushes as she made her way to her work across the street as a housemaid. Leaps Up, who had been following her, turned back with a whimper at Takota's command.

When she returned, the sun was sending shadows in the opposite direction. It had been a long, tedious day of endless chores, it seemed. As she enterd upon the path to the cabin, Anpaytoo was startled by voices, louder than usual, invading the usually quiet space outside the door. Hantaywee and Tokala Kohana could be heard in the other room vying with Takota's gruff, low voice.

"Tasunke Paytah must come with us. We cannot leave him here. He has done no wrong. We cannot send him alone into exile." Takota insisted, reiterating the Dakota code.

"How long must we wait? Forever? We have been waiting for him since I was a little boy. I have seen the winters come and go, and with each snowfall, my shadow grows longer." Tokala Kohana shouted, his voice cracking. "I am now fully grown. I can wait no longer."

"I will go into town tomorrow to get him," said Takota. "Then we can leave together."

At that Anpaytoo appeared at the doorway. They stopped arguing. "So everything was yes, yes this morning. So agreeable when I was here, but now?" she said. Hantaywee walked over to stir the pot of stew on the stove, and Takota left to retrieve more meat from the shed that served as a larder. When he returned, except for the scraping of chairs and clinking of utensils, they ate their meal in silence. Anpaytoo noticed the frown lines that deepened between Hantawee's eyes and Takota's befuddled look, not having at least thanked Wankan Tanka, the four leggeds and winged creatures that made the meal possible. He stared ruefully at his son, Tokala Kohana, who ate with a grudging air, looking from mother to father as if he didn't know them very well, until now. His thin, aquiline nose, sharp eyes and set of his mouth, mirrored the face of his father.

The bell on the other side of the river sounded and summoned Tokala Kohana to pull the chains of the big flatbed boat back and forth across the waters whenever travelers approached. Hantaywee made preparations to finish her work in the garden, knowing that when they had some free time, she and her son would wade into the river, spearing fish for other meals. With high spirits, Anpaytoo followed her with a basket for harvesting that she bent her strong body towards, plucking, pulling and lifting vegetables until the sunset bruised the sky that covered it with stars in the dark.

16

AN IMPEDIMENT

The next morning lifted the curtain of darkness, spilling a fine sheen of light onto the river and throughout their rooms. The cabin became alive with the family's morning preparations, including each one's prayer to the four directions at the riverside. After breakfast, Takota walked with Anpaytoo, followed by Leaps Up, until they reached the street and Hantaywaee could be heard, calling the dog with an offer of leftovers from their morning meal. Both father and daughter shared a deep sense of foreboding as they approached the different worlds of the white man. They parted company when she strolled across the street, dressed in gingham and leather shoes, her hair brushed back in a bun, ready to enter into the home of the widower from the far off country of Poland, while Takota's only gesture of acceptance of the white man's world was the hat he wore, embellished with a feather. In his buckskins and moccasins, his tall, lurking figure made a strange sight as he strode down the walk into town.

Oblivious to the horse carts and carriages on the streets, the shops and small gatherings of well-dressed dwellers; Takota had one thing in mind – to bring Tasunke Paytah home. In a sense, he admired his son and daughter, their ability to adapt to a world that left him bewildered. But as they moved into their roles with apparent ease, he knew that they would never fit in no matter how hard they tried. Tasunke Paytah must come with him even though he seemed trapped in a society where his strength had become essential enough to command a certain amount of the white man's money and respect. *When would they ever stop building? Takota thought. Well, that didn't matter. When he told his son about Troubled Spirit, he would leave the glamour of the city to return to the old ways, to return to the lessons of mother earth. Of that Takota was sure.*

It was the day the Polish people called "Sunday." Church bells gonged twelve times and the sun was directly overhead when he stopped in front of a shantytown apartment building, pushed open the gray wooden door and ascended the creaking stairs. The door with the number 326 was slightly ajar, but he knocked anyway until he had to push it open. Tasunke Paytah was lying on a cot next to the far wall, his bare chest moving with the breath of sleep. A whisky bottle and two shot glasses were on the table where he had left them. Takota approached the table and examined the glasses, one with a lipstick imprint on it. He turned toward the small iron wood stove, walked over, opened the packet that Hantaywee had given him and dumped the pieces of rabbit, carrots and potatoes into a pot he filled with water from a jug nearby. The food was warm but the smell of the pink meat was fresh. It needed to be cooked over the fire he started with a few more chunks of wood. As if it were a campfire, he fanned the stove's flames.

Then he drew near to his son, lying on a dingy sheet draped over the cot. "Wake up, Tasunke Paytah!" Takota shook his son out of a stupor until he opened his groggy eyes, sat up, shook his head, and leaned back on his elbows. His swarthy face and torso were florid with pock mark scars, yet bore the pallid undertone of malnourishment.

"You!" he said, his voice still hoarse with sleep. "What are you doing here?"

"I've come to take you with us. It's not safe for us here anymore."

"Not safe?" He sat up at the edge of the cot, pushed back his long black hair, parting it into several grooves with his fingers, and laughed until his voice caught and his face flushed with the effort. "When have we ever been safe?

Takota sat down next to him to tell him the story of Troubled Spirit and how he had died. After which, the young brave, yawned, stood up and stretched, leaning a little; with an unsteady gait, he approached the table and sat on a chair. He picked up one of the two shot glasses next to the bottle, which he opened, and poured himself a drink before he offered some to his father. The floor creaked while Takota walked over, stood behind him and placed his hands on his son's shoulders, which felt bony and wasted, not as muscular and strong as they once were.

"That fire water will kill you," he muttered before he sat down at the table, and stared at his son, wondering how he was going to persuade him to leave this place.

"Nah, it's good stuff. Here," said Tasunke Paytah who poured a shot in the other glass and pushed it across the table to his father, who looked at it with disgust.

"I never liked that stuff. It's too bitter."

"Like bitter medicine, eh? One of the great gifts of the wasi'chu!" His son downed the whiskey in the shot glass he had given Takota, shook his head and grimaced, exhaling. "So I take it, just like I take their money for every tree they cut down. They are our trees that they cut down and saw through at the lumber mill. The white man owes us that much."

"How long will you be claiming this payment? Takota eyed him with skepticism.

"For as long as I can." Tasunke Paytah leaned back, his eyes glazed with a strange, slumbering fury. "If you want me to go back with you, back to the old ways, I'll tell you that the old ways don't exist anymore. They are gone along with the forests, the deer, bear, raccoon, beaver, and all the others in the woods that used to live with us. The fish are dying too. The earth is becoming like an old woman, dried up and covered with sores, covered with the sickness the wasi'chu brings." He poured himself another shot. Takota watched this strange dance of death with the white man's ways – one minute taking payment for the very destruction his son was helping them achieve, another minute, drinking their poison for the few brief moments it dulled his agonizing pain.

Tasunke Pahtah leaned his broad face forward with his chest against the table and eyed Takota. "You know we had a war and we almost won." His husky voice rose with excitement.

Takota nodded, "How could I not know when we were in the middle of it?"

"We beat them at Redwood Ferry. We wiped them out at Milford, Leavenworth and Sacred Heart and burned down most of New Ulm. We held back Fort Ridgely, raided settlements, and defeated the militia at Birch Coulee. Settlers weren't safe along the Red River Trails in their fancy stagecoaches and on their ferries. They fled to Fort Abercrombie, but we attacked them there, too. We were everywhere and we were winning." Tasunke Paytah's deep voice trailed off.

"I know. I was there," said his father.

"You?"

Takota nodded. "I was a scout. Our attacks were planned based on what I saw and reported to the warrior councils."

"All this time I thought you stayed with Hantaywee, Anpaytoo, Tokala Kohana, and me."

"I travelled back and forth." Tokala said, setting the record straight. "I was the one who ran for many miles to the council, warning them about the seventh regiment with their canon that the white man's President

Lincoln had sent to defeat us. That's why some of us split off and traveled up north on the Great River where we settled."

"I didn't know." Tasunke propped his elbows on the table and clutched his hands.

Takota grabbed his arm. "There's a lot you don't know, son." He said with a gruff yet gentle tone in his voice. "For one thing, we're not supposed to be here." Takota spoke earnestly. "The settlers and their father in Washington took everything we ever had, using our battle as an excuse when all we were doing was reclaiming what they had taken from us. We could have lived together, but they wanted to see us die in the fields like starved dogs. And now they have made us exiles in our own land"

He released his son's arm. "When they came here, we let them use our territory. When they began to push us out of their way, we asked for payment. When they refused to pay and would not even share the fruits of the earth with us, would not even give us enough from their bins of grain to save us from starvation, and then told us to eat grass, we had enough. We decided it was time to drive them out. We became the fire burning away the blight that they had become."

"We could have stopped them long ago with Tecumseh." Paytah broke in while he looked up. "From what I heard from Iroquois who were passing through here, he was reviving the old confederacies we had before him – the Iroquois, the Pequots and Mohicans, the three confederacies down South, the Creeks, Natchez and Powhattan."

Takota nodded. "That is old history. Throughout it all, we made fatal mistakes. Here, in Minnesota, you say we beat them at New Ulm, but that was a hollow victory and only after we lost much from bad timing. I was there when Little Crow pleaded with them to attack Fort Ridgely first when it was weakened by the loss of Captain Marsh and half his men after we ambushed them. Then, Ridgely was held by only twenty-four soldiers under young Lieutenant Gere, who would have been too green to hold it. The Fort would have supplied us with food, blankets, six cannon, our annuities of $71,000 in gold. Even Big Eagle said, 'the fort was the door to the valley as far as to Kaposia (St. Paul), and if we got through the door, nothing could stop us this side of the Mississippi.'"

Tasunke Paytah looked down and shook his head, reflecting on his father's knowledge.

Takota continued. "New Ulm was a mistake. By the time we got back to Fort Ridgely, Gere was replaced with the older, more experienced Lieutenant Sheehan who had arrived with over 200 men. Then we attacked in the middle of rain storms and our flaming arrows splattered against their drenched buildings. They formed a unit and hit us with rifle fire, and even though we drove them back, they drove us away with their twelve to twenty-four pound guns that mowed us down with massive shots of hot, dirty bullets. Yes, we won at New Ulm, driving away thousands, as one of their commanders said, we came down on that town 'like a windstorm.'

But we needed Fort Ridgely."

"You don't understand," Tasunke Paytah said. "You expect me to come with you, and return to the old ways, which are gone. Face it, the hairy-faced wasi'chu has destroyed our forests to build these square houses that they prowl around in like animals in a cage. They've driven away and killed the game that we used to hunt, and the rivers and streams are dying, filled with their flatboats and refuse. Even the water birds are not returning."

They both sat in empty silence, staring at the wood grain of the table top.

"The old ways are still here," Takota muttered. "If you had come with us when I first asked you to, we would be living as we did before."

"Where? To the West with the white man in hot pursuit, killing everyone who gets in the way of their greed for gold? Or maybe we could go back and live along the East Coast where they drove out many tribes? Or maybe to the South where they plunder each other and trample the tribes underfoot in the process?" Tasunke Paytah, shook his head and glared ar his father.

,"Grandmother's Land, you know, the country the white man calls Canada," Takota said with a toss of his head.

His disgruntled son looked away. "What makes you think the white man won't find us there?"

"Not as many of them go there, and some Dakota have settled around Lake Winnipeg. They've made arrangements with the Ojibwy for the use of Rainy River. Game and fish are plentiful. You could find yourself a nice Dakota woman, not one of those cheap, painted tavern whores." He nodded at the stained shot glass. "You could be part of a tiospaye, a tribe, a better life. And we would be together again."

"I've heard it's a hard life up there, and the winters are fierce."

"When have we ever had an easy life?" Takota asked. "And tell me, how easy is for you here? Do you want to live this way, jumping up when the white man calls? Or would you rather greet each day at the water's edge, honoring the four directions? reading the signs of the earth that lead you to your next meal? coaxing the women's crops to grow and knowing when and where they will thrive? finding the roots and berries where the land supplies them?"

"I remember when the Ojibway traded us their marshland rice and we ate it with meat."

"And tanned the deer hides for our tipis, jackets, leggings and moccasins. Dakota women would do that and they would know how to roast the meat with vegetables – just so." Tasunke Paytah looked into Takota's eyes, threw back his head and laughed, looked down to recover his seriousness and looked up at his father. "All this time we've been giving furs and land in treaties to the white man when what they really needed were meals cooked by Dakota women." He shook his head. "You have me there, except for one thing."

"And what's that?"

"I have to finish the job."

"Can't they find someone else?"

"They could, but then there would be a delay in their delivery and they would raise holy hell, come after me, and make trouble for us. I can't let that happen."

"How long will it take?"

"A few moons."

"You know, it is now spring and a good time to travel. We don't want to go up north in the winter." Takota walked over to the stove and ladled the rabbit stew into a couple of bowls Tasunke Pahtah had stashed in the cupboard. Having retrieved the meal and a few utensils, his father returned to the table.

His son looked up, ran his hands through his disheveled hair and smiled. "Two moons and I'll be leaving with you. That will give us plenty of time to get there before the snows fall."

"Before even the leaves fall," Takota agreed, wolfing down the soup while he watched his estranged son do the same. When he finished, he felt weary and looked around the room, noticing the shadows lengthening across the floor. He stood up and walked over to gaze out the dingy window onto the street below. "It's getting late," he said. "I'd better get going." The bells from the church tower, resounding throughout the settlement, confirmed his observation that it was late afternoon.

Tasunke Paytah was at his side, pressing a pouch of coins and bills into his hand. "Take this. It will help you get through the next few moons."

"But you need it," Takota objected.

"Nah. I will have enough from where that came from." For a brief moment, Tasunke Paytah seemed to have become the energetic, caring young brave that he once was, but before Takota left, he turned to glance at this son and caught sight of him again, sitting at the table, his silhouette fading into the shadows of the afternoon, a defeated, sad and lonely figure. *Will I ever have my son back? he thought.*

17

THE WAITING GAME

(Medicine Lodge Treaty – October 28, 1867; Battle of Little Big Horn – June 25-26, 1876)

Hantaywee cried out with a wailing chant when she saw Takota standing in the doorway without Tasunke Paytah. Anpaytoo and Tokala Kohana rushed into the kitchen while Takota wearily sat down at the table where a candle was lit, its light sending shadows across his face. "He will be coming with us, but we have to wait a few moons," he said.

"Wait?" Tokala Kohana shouted. Agitated, he walked about the room, his fringed deerskin shirt and leggings rustling in time with his footsteps while Leaps Up stood, alert and growling, brown and black hairs bristling. "I have already waited half my life for him. I will wait no longer." He placed his strong hands flat on the table and glared fiercely into Takota's distressed eyes.

Takota glanced away and placed the money pouch on the table where he sat with his head down. “He gave us this to help us through the next few moons until he will be able to join us.”

“So that’s why you went to him,” Tokala Kohana shouted, straightened, stood back. His veins stood out on his face while he glared at Takota. “You will never leave. You’ve grown too soft. You’d rather use the white man’s money to buy food than to hunt and fish and dig for it. You’d rather have Anpaytoo wear their calico than our tanned hides. Look at you with that white man’s hat and eagle feather. You never wanted to leave.” Takota lifted his hand to object, but then rested his head on it while Hantaywee sat next to him and took his other hand in hers.

“While you were gone I ferried a Dakota hunting party from across the river,” Kohana continued. “They are on their way to Grandmother’s Land (Canada) and told me where to meet them if we want to go with them. I’m going, and nothing can stop me. I will leave when the sun rises.” He turned and entered the back rooms to pack his things.

Before starting after Tokala Kohana, Anpaytoo took a quick glance at her mother and father, sitting at the table together, their hands clasped, while they gazed at each other through weary eyes settling into wrinkles, their dark hair, turning grey with white streaks of hair framing their faces. They were beginning to look old and tired, she thought. “Wait,” she whispered through her teeth as she entered into the darkness and grabbed Tokala Kohana’s arm. “What are you doing? Don’t you see, we all must go together?”

He turned and held her by the shoulders. "This is the only chance I we'll ever get." He motioned his head in the direction of the kitchen. "They'll never leave. Come with me, Anpaytoo, Chayton Enapay, the brave who loves you, is waiting for you. We can begin a new life together. As for that brother of ours," he said while releasing her and turning away, "He's no longer Tasunke Paytah to me." With that he left her alone in the darkness where she listened to him as he rummaged in the shadows, lighted only by shafts of moonlight.

"But we can't leave them. They're getting old and need our help. We must stay together." Her words were met with silence and rustling sounds as he prepared for his journey.

When Tokala Kohana left without a sound in the early morning dawn before anyone awoke, the promise of spring seemed to have gone with him. Oh, the garden beds glistened in the sun with their budding life as did the trees, filled with birds' songs, and bait fish could be found in schools along the river. But even the sun could not erase how dismal Anpaytoo felt over the absence of her brother. A grey pall seemed to have fallen over the newly forming life, matched only by the rain which pelted their home and replenished the river moving relentlessly under its grey sheen. Her tears were backed up in her eyes, but they were falling inside her heart that she held close so that she could care for her father and mother with a cheerful demeanor.

"We will soon join Kohana," Takota said, approaching her in the garden one day where weeding was her routine. She stood and gave him a morose look. "A few moons and we'll be gone from here," he assured her. All the while, he was aware of warning signs; their neighbors seemed to have grown aloof; not as many of them used the ferry; and he recalled one day as he was returning from the trader's, a short, scruffy member of a group of men, gathered on the corner, shouted out at him.

"Hey Injun! Where's your boss?" the man sneered and with a rough cough, spat on the walk. "Hey!" The stranger persisted, while he stood defiantly facing him from across the street with his face set in a grimace and his eyes narrow with hate. Takota kept walking, but they continued with sneers and cat calls. Exasperated, he stopped and faced them from across the street.

"He's on a journey." He shouted, standing tall with courage coursing through every fiber of his being, his shirt flapping in the wind.

"Oh yeah? Well, he's been gone a long time, too long," said another, brawny, stalwart member, who also spat on the road and glared at him. Takota continued walking, a feeling of foreboding spreading through him like a cold chill, knowing that they knew. He began to mull over the news he'd overheard at the Trading Post that day where the men chewed tobacco around the stove, told stories and harangued about how the settlers had cleared Minnesota of its Sioux Indians, but that wasn't enough. The men rested against posts, smoked pipes and cigars and sat in wicker chairs, warming up to their subjects.

"Our army," said one of them while he cleared his throat, "rounded up the Indians on the plains a couple of years ago, down south of us – a lot of Comanche, Kiowa, Cheyenne, and Arapaho — mainly in the Texas Panhandle."

"Yeah but the Injuns held out with raids and skirmishes," countered another gruff voice, "We lost a lotta men there, until General Sheridan's troops attacked 'em with five columns of troops along the Red River." He gripped a Pony Express paper that retold the story of the Texas wars. "With relentless forays," he read, "the federal troops captured the tribes and drove them into two reservations as ordered by the Medicine LodgeTreaty." He gripped the paper down at his side. "If you ask me, I think that's too good for them dirty redskins." The men growled with their angry assent.

Takota recalled how he had walked past them and stepped outside with such stealth that the men hadn't notice him. He felt as if he had escaped a nest of rattlesnakes about to strike. He knew in his heart that even though the Polish settlers around him were biding their time, their wrath was simmering. His remembered his Cheyenne friends and other nations who were in trouble, just as the Sioux were, and wars were raging across the plains, he mused, wondering where to go next. He glanced at the settlement, its rows of houses, lining both sides of the streets where there once was a vast and almost impenetrable forest. In the distance he saw that he was nearing the hedges that surrounded Griswald's place, the shelter of security and laughter that was becoming insecure and even dangerous. His wife and children's safety was foremost on his mind as he trudged toward the old cabin. His legs ached from the long walk, and his heart was reeling over the surly news from the trading post.

When he turned toward the walkway of the house, he saw Anpaytoo strolling across the street from old man Casmir's. As she passed a group of men on the corner, they gave her a look that made Takota shudder, but Anpayto hadn't noticed for she had eyes only for him. His daughter, he thought, was as loyal as her mother. She did not leave with Tokala Kohana, but worked hard at Casmir's and brought home the white man's filthy money, he thought, money he would not need in Grandmother's Land (Canada). He sighed. The second moon would soon be over. And then they would be leaving. He watched Anapaytoo wend toward him, her face radiant in the summer sun. When she reached him, they ambled down the long pathway and into the house together where Hantaywee awaited their return.

18

WHAT TAKOTA DIDN'T KNOW

What Takota didn't know, though, was the game Anpaytoo was forced to play with Casmir's lanky, lecherous son, Zeke, who dropped by Casmir's house every once in awhile to see his father. Everything about Zeke was angular, sleek and slithery, from his tough, big-boned frame to his dirty blonde hair, slicked back. Though Casmir had introduced him in an almost off handed way, her instincts were aroused by his stealthy approach during her first encounter alone with him, That was when one of her tasks took place in the basement of the house where she scrubbed the laundry on the washboard propped up in the grey, cement laundry sink, shortly after she had served breakfast, and Casmir had left for work. It was gloomy and yet, the light streamed through a small window onto the dark, dank cement walls, obscuring the hulking shadow of the man who crept up behind her. But she was alert enough to feel his presence, and her heart leapt up as she turned and threw the wet clothes she gripped into his face. Trembling with fright, she raced passed the bulky edges of the old coal furnace and stumbled up the stairs, out the door and into the garden where she began humming while she knelt in the dirt to do her daily ritual of weeding and tending the plants, but she was clammy with sweat and a racing heart.

"I'll get you yet," Zeke shouted through thick lips as he lumbered past the gate, leering at her with his small eyes squinting under his heavy brows, and strode toward his house down the street where his wife and children lived.

Ever after, she laundered the clothes in the evening while Casmir was at home, eating his dinner. She would leave the clothes basket by the basement door and would hang the laundry on the line in the morning. Zeke was Casmir's son; she dared not tell his father how he scared her.

"Why don't you sit with me like you used to, dziewcyna?" Casmir would ask. "I want to see you and talk with you."

Casmir was a decrepit, old man, although in actual years he could have been considered middle aged. But he lived for momentary pleasures — the distraction of his work as a bookkeeper at the mills, the warmth of the beer, whiskey and hearty meals he would imbibe, the joviality of his card playing cronies – all of which served as a veneer over the deep loss and loneliness he refused to confront. His round, Slavic face with its pale blue eyes, which stared out in sad, pouched circles over his rotund cheeks, bulbous nose and pursed mouth, belied the long life's journey he had already taken. He was a hefty man, well built, yet betraying an inner decadence in his slovenly shuffle, dull gaze and slack mouth. His sandy hair grew in abundance on his cheeks and brows, but thinned at the top, giving him a domed forehead. With some coaxing from his late wife, he managed to grow a respectable mustache and beard and to comb his hair back. A gentleman farmer, who had reached New York with enough money in his pockets from the sale of his land in the "old country" to purchase land here, he arrived with his pregnant wife, Anastasia, who had been devastated by the rough Atlantic crossing.

It was while he was overseeing the construction of their new home here in the Minnesota hinterlands and while she was living at the midwife's that he lost her. The wife he lovingly called Anna died while giving birth to Zeke in this strange land where Indians still appeared as if from nowhere. He was drawn to the pretty young Dakota housekeeper, yet something in Casmir could not accept Anpaytoo's heritage nor say her foreign sounding name, Anpaytoo, and so he called her *dziewcyna* (young girl) and a shortened name that he coined for his comfort.

"Anya, please, come here and sit with me," he pleaded, pulling out a chair. She complied, except for that one day a week when she had to worry about his son and disrupt the breakfast routine.

"I like to get things ready ahead of time," she had told him, referring to the wash while she sat down with a smile and poured them cups of tea, all the while longing to return to the safety of her family across the street. The ramshackle cabin where they lived had indeed become home to her, where the river seemed to bask in the summer sun and the light of the full moon. She held it in her mind's eye, while the warm west winds swept through the cabin, bringing with it the scent of wildflowers and vegetation. Leaps Up chose their porch to sleep on, and they fed him what scraps they could. So comical, her family would laugh together, eating their flapjacks in the sunny kitchen, throwing pieces to Leaps Up.

Takota also did not know that during one night of the full moon, Hantaywee approached their daughter, standing on the riverbank in the silver of the moonlight. "Why did you not tell me about this?" Hantaywee held out a piece of cloth splattered with blood.

Anpaytoo turned away and looked down at her hands. "I, I didn't know what to say; I didn't know what it was. Then it went away." She looked up at her mother.

"Oh my daughter, it means that you are becoming a full-grown woman. You are one with the movements of the moon now, a special gift to women." Wistful, she shook her head. "If we were with our tribe, you would have known and then would take part in the ceremony for young maidens like you." She paused for awhile, looked at her daughter, smiled and embraced her. Thoughts raced through her head about the proper upbringing of a daughter as lovely as Anpaytoo. "I will have to plan a celebration before the next moon, so that you will know how close we are to our generous mother earth who keeps us alive. We, too, can be fruitful and replenish the land."

The next morning, the mother addressed Wakan Tanka, the Great Mystery, as she stood at the water's edge and with sprinkles of tobacco she sent her messages to the four directions, ending with this plea: "I am at the meeting point where the roads cross, and it is sacred," she said. "My daughter is becoming a young woman in a strange place; oh hear me, Wankan Tanka, and keep her on the sacred way as were the women before her. Oh help me to guide her, for I must be her Wisdom Keeper now."

That evening, having caught fish, gathered herbs in the meadows and harvested some vegetables from the garden so she could feed her family during the day, she returned at sunset for her ritual at the riverside and brought Anya with her. They were both dressed in buckskin and stood barefoot in the river as she recalled the "Ishna Ta Awi Cha Lowan" (Her Alone They Sing Over) ceremony for her daughter. Hantawee began to marvel at the waning moon surrounded by shimmering stars with its mysterious hold on all that lived.

"See this rising moon, daughter," she said. "Because you are a woman, you are one with its power over the tides and the seasons in the great circle of life. You must know your part in this life, and it is sacred. When you bear children and raise them to follow the sacred path, you must understand that you are like the Mother Earth who also is fruitful. In the ceremony, you will be honored in this way – After you are purified in the Inipi (Sweat Lodge), Takota will present you to the holy medicine man, our Wicasa. He will have built a separate tipi for you where you will stay and receive food that will be brought to you. Holy women will teach you what your duties are as a woman. Wicasa will pray over you with the sacred pipe and plead with the powers of the four directions, asking the Spirit of the West to strengthen you and the generations that follow you, asking for help during your red and blue days. He will beg the giant Waziak, Power of the North, to send good health and purifying winds. From the rising sun of the East he will ask for wisdom and from the White Swan of the South, power over your sacred path for generations to come, so that all of you may walk in a sacred manner." Hantaywee stopped, trying to remember the ritual as she had experienced it. "Then Wicasa will hold some tobacco up to call on Wakan Tanka and our four relatives: Grandfather, Father, Grandmother, and Mother, " Hantaywee continued, holding her arm up, showing how he would hold it. "Wicasa will call on the sacred power of Tatanka, the buffalo. He will blow red smoke on you like the buffalo cow does on her calf, only he will do it six times, and he will purify himself and a stone hatchet with sweet grass smoke. Then with the hatchet he will dig out a hollow in the ground at the center of the tipi where he will put some tobacco and with it will draw a line from West to East and from North to South and the lines will cross. Over it he will paint a blue line, showing that heaven (the blue line) and earth (the tobacco) are one."

Hantaywee moved closer to Anpaytoo and spoke at almost a whisper. "You know how sacred the buffalo is to us. Well, Wicasa will put a buffalo skull facing east on the earth mound near the hollow and will paint a red line around its head and a straight line between its horns and down its forhead. Then he'll put sage in the skull's eyes and a wooden bowl of the sacred water of life with sweet red cherries in front of the skull's mouth. The cherries represent us, the red people. All this is very wakan (sacred)."

"Then he will make a bundle containing sweet grass, a piece of bark from a Cherry tree, and some hair from a buffalo. You will stand and hold the bundle over your head so that you will know that Wakan Tanka (the Great Spirit) is above you – between heaven and earth. You will now be the tree of life and you and your generations from you will be holy. Every step you take will be sacred and you will be a great influence. While Wicasa will rub you with the bundle he will call upon the four powers of the universe to purify you. Then you will sit with the relatives there to hear him tell you the story of the buffalo. You will drink four sips of the sacred water of life and eat a piece of purified buffalo meat. Before you leave, Wicasa will honor you as someone who will be humble, fruitful, and generous like Mother Earth. After a traditional dance, song, prayer and instructions, you will leave the tipi – no longer thought to be a girl, but a woman. Others will want to touch you because you will be holy. Then there will be a feast and a 'give away.'" (Hantawee remembered this from the great Medicine Man, Black Elk)

Anpaytoo listened and remembered all that her mother had told her. When they returned that evening, her heart was singing, "I am sacred; I am the tree of life."

Everyday, Hantaywee tended the garden in earnest, cultivating it from spring lettuce and squash to summer tomatoes and pole beans. She felt the fresh soil in her hands and marveled over the multitude of seeds she gathered for the next crop. Their larder was always full, and even though Tasunke Paytah's bag of coins had been used up, Anpaytoo's steady earnings kept them living well. At the same time, Hantaywee realized that they would have to return to see Wicasa to give Anpaytoo a proper ceremony. She tried to approach Takota about it, but his mind was preoccupied with other problems.

"Go to Wicasa? Why? Oh, the woman ceremony. I don't know how we can do that for we must be gone for more than a day." Takota would say and walk away, headed toward town where he would stand at the entryway to the local trading store, staring longingly in the direction of Tasunke Paytah's place, often on the brink of trudging those few miles on the hot streets to find him again and make him leave this place where the tension over their presence was growing tighter every day, like an overwound spring about to be released. He could see it in the eyes of those who watched him enter the store; he could feel it in the storekeeper's voice whenever he made a purchase.

19

OMINOUS SIGNS

As usual, Tokata approached the counter. "Is this for Griswald?" Ben asked, now aging with a head of grey hair and a grizzled beard. He slapped down the goods with an impatient briskness while Takota nodded. The rustling, coughing, and scuffing behind him indicated to Takota that the neighbors were not taking kindly to this Dakota, who, were it not for his friend and employer, Griswald, would have been driven away long ago. Before he left, he turned and tarried a little at the back of the store to listen to words that hit him like fiery bullets.

"Them damn fool Injuns done wiped out our finest regiment!" spat out one of the men while shooting his spittle into a spittoon. "Killed our greatest injun fighter, Colonel Custer, at Little Big Horn and some 270 men from the Seventh Regiment"

"Lemme see that," said another who grabbed the *Pony Express News* that crinckled in dry air around the stove. "What the hell!" he exclaimed.

"Says the Crow scouts estimated about 800 Injuns, but there really were close to 7,000 or more... Outnumbered Custer's troops three to one..."

"Eh! They needed another zero. But those Crow scouts couldn't count higher than 100 anyway..." one of the men snorted. The men's voices rumbled with consent.

The reader held up his hand for silence. "The notice goes on to say that the military had a fail proof plan. They sent three battalions with eight companies: Col. Custer commanded two battalions with five companies while Col. Reno commanded the third battalion with three companies. These eight companies were the main force. Col. Benteen and three companies went to the south to reinforce the main advance. A final company with special soldiers from the other regiments made up the rear guard and a pack-train with supplies."

"That makes over twelve companies," a young man's voice interjected from the rear.

"Damn good plan!" One of the men said.

"Straight outta the book," said another, wagging his head while chawing tobacco over his mug of spirits.

"So Custer's was the hammer and Reno's was the anvil," said another experienced Civil War fighter

"But is seems like them Injuns just...just," the reader shook his head in bewilderment,

"clobbered 'em."

"You mean ambushed?"

"No, charged at Custer and his men like they was..was buffalo." The reader dropped the paper on the table and walked away. Another man picked it up and read, "And then the warriors mutilated them…" The grumbling among the men grew harsh and loud. "Them damn Injuns! Gonna shoot 'em on sight!"

At that, Tokala slipped out the door. *I don't want to be here anymore than you do,* he thought when he saw the neighbors glower at him. *Just give me back my son, and we will go to a much better place. It will soon be too late,* he thought one day while watching the lengthening shadows of the third moon of the summer. *We may have to wait another winter here.* And then he wondered, *why have I let the southern winds put me into a dreamless sleep? Why do I awaken daily to unfulfilled desires? To feel hopeless, lost, and unable to move, as if my feet were pushing against deep sand in a pit that impedes my path?*

Entwined among these concerns were the pleas of Hantaywee to plan a woman's ceremony for Anpaytoo. I will go to Wicasa, he thought. He felt as if he were in a windstorm at times with Anpaytoo's laughter in the swaying trees sighing and almost singing while Tasunke Paytah's sad moan seemed to arise with the surly torrents that would follow the dark clouds gathering above. Hantaywee would be there in the doorway, calling him into the comfort of her arms and the soft, mellow glow of the wood stove fire. But there was always the threat of Father Lincoln's decree to drive the Dakotas out of Minnesota, which sent chills down his spine.

As the enclave of Polish immigrants increased around him, he wondered why he grasped at what little was left of the old ways. After all, most of the deer had vanished; rabbits were their fare now, while the immigrants ate beef imported from the plains. The fish were much harder to find in the great river, and the few that he caught were thin and wasted.

Yet, he felt that he had at least accomplished something – he had kept Hantaywee and Anpaytoo safe from the wars across the plains and the wantoness of the wasi'chus around them. He assured himself of that each morning when he greeted the four directions with scattered tobacco grains while he stood by the river, with his pipe and turned, chanting, until, finally, he addressed Wankon Tanka, at his center, that Sacred Place where he was one with the universe.

"Grandfather, Wakan Tanka, though my voice is weak, hear me! May I walk upon the Red Road in this Circle of Life and follow the path you made for me among the two-legged, four-legged, the winged ones and all living plants – all that belong to you."

Then he repeated a chant from memory: "You have made the spirits of the four parts of the earth cross each other. You have made me go across the good road and the hard road, and where they cross, is a holy place. You are the life everywhere, everyday." He turned to face the day before him, to run the ferry, fish when he could and hunt rabbits, anticipating when Tasunke Paytah would show up at their door, ready to leave with them. *This I do know, he thought.*

But what he did not know one morning while he worked the ferry, was that Anpaytoo arrived at Casmir's and saw that the laundry basket was not by the door to the basement. She fed the old man breakfast, but anxiously rushed around while in the back of her mind, she tried to figure out how she would fetch the laundry.

"Where must it be?" she murmured.

"Must what be?" Casmir asked while about to leave.

"The laundry" She laughed. "Would you wait for me while I look for it?" She opened the door to the basement, hurrying down the stairs.

Meanwhile, she found it, hidden in a far corner of the basement. "Here it is," she shouted back, relieved until she heard voices upstairs and the front door slam. By then she was almost at the top of the stairs, carrying the heavy basket in front of her when she looked up and saw Zeke, smirking at her, blocking the way. She broke out in a cold sweat, backed down, her entire body, shaking, hurriedly looked around and spied the basement window, when she heard Casmir's voice.

"Why are you standing there, Zeke? I told you the tool you're looking for is in the shed."

He pushed Zeke aside and peered down the steps. "Anya, I hear your mother crying out. Something's gone wrong over there."

20

THE AFTERMATH

{1876—Lakota/Cheyenne Wars)

When he heard Hantaywee's wail, Takota pulled the chains of the ferry, propelling him from the west bank, where the customers had disembarked, and back to the east bank. He strained at the chains and landed the flatbed boat at a speed which he hadn't thought possible, as she ran. At the same time, Anpaytoo raced around the corner of the bushes at the walkway and, as shr ran toward the front of the house, saw Hantaywee, sobbing over a bundle in her arms.

As she, herself, ran toward them, Anpaytoo saw Takota reach the top of the bank and rush into the clearing where he met Hantaywee who was running toward him, carrying Leaps Up. The three of them came together around the slain pet.

"You had to wait," she muttered, glaring at him. He took one look at the dog, who had been shot and killed, but not until after he had been tortured and mangled. While gardening, Hantaywee explained, she had heard a thump and found him, thrown onto their porch.

"We will wait no longer. I will go to Tasunke Paytah and bring him back, even if I haveto drag him." Takota cried out. With that, he turned, bolted out the porch, ran down the path and headed toward town. He ran so fast, he felt like he was a young scout, racing to the chief with news. The city came into view and the buildings were nothing more than brown blurs as he dashed past them. He heard the clop of horses pulling wagons down the street, but he didn't see them for the wind was in his eyes and he was staring straight ahead, intent upon his purpose, all the while knowing that he could not flee the sick feeling of foreboding at the pit of his stomach.

Takota was sweating and breathing heavily when he pounded on the door to 326. Dilapidated as it was, it gave in, showing a disheveled Tasunke Paytah, who sat up on the edge of his cot, his emaciated body wracked with sickness.

"What do you want from me old man?" he muttered while he bent over, eying his father from under his black brows, his large, bony hands on his knees.

"I want you to come with me – now. You're the only one holding us back."

"Well, then go without me." He lowered his head and ran his hands through his long black hair.

"Oh, you foolish boy! Where is the brave I raised from an infant, gave a name and life?"

Tacota walked over to his son, sat down next to him and touched him, noticing his sagging skin, his thin body, the red marks on his neck and abdomen, and that he was burning with fever. He drew close and whispered in his ear. At that Tasunke Paytah sat upright.

"Who is it that did this? I will find him and I will kill him." He arose to his feet, but his legs buckled under him and he sat back onto the cot again.

Takota found a large muslin drawstring bag in the closet that he filled with Tasunke Paytah's things and proceeded to help him up. "Lean on me," he said, but realized, after they had managed a few steps forward, that his son was almost a dead weight. He could barely move his legs, much less walk. Takota proceeded to lift and drag him across the room to the open doorway, bungling down the stairs, out and onto the walkway. Tasunke Paytah slumped and slid down into a sitting position next to the entrance, unable to move forward. A group of men across the road watched with faint amusement.

A passerby shouted out from across the roadway, "Ain't that injun dead yet?"

A man separated from the group, crossed the street, approached, and greeted Tacota. "He with you?" he asked in a soft voice, motioning toward

Tasunke Paytah. When Takota nodded, the tall, thin bespectacled Polish gentleman with graying hair introduced himself as Dr. Ed Kasminski. "And you?"

"I'm Takota Wahchinskapa (Wise Friend), Tasunke Paytah's father."

"Paytah? Everyone around here calls him Peter, Pete for short. He's been sick for a long time now; from those red spots it looks like typhoid, we call it. There's been some cases at the mills where he works. Stuff can spread like wildfire; I keep telling the owners to clean up their workplace. Any decent company would see to that." When he saw the bewildered look on Takota's face, he turned and yelled at one of the men in the group, "Hey Frank, bring me my wagon will yah?" One of the men, tall and tow headed, split from the group and disappeared around the corner. After a long wait, he reappeared, driving a horse and wagon.

"That's my son," said Dr. Kasminski. "Let's put your son, Paytah, in my wagon and get him home where he can die in peace."

21

A DREAM IS DEFERRED

While waiting for the tea to steep, Hantaywee, seated at the kitchen table, had fallen asleep, her head resting on her folded arms; the evening dusk had fallen and a candle glowed in the middle of the table. Anpaytoo paced back and forth, thinking fondly of Tasuke Pahtah and Tokala Kohana with whom she fished and hunted and had so many adventures with wildlife. She watched over her mother, noticing her silver hair threaded through the black strands and glimmering in the sparse light. Awakened by the noise of the three men supporting Tasunke Paytah, who groaned and stumbled with them down the pathway, Hantaywee arose, picked up the candle in its boat-like holder and shone its light on the doorway where she and Anpaytoo stood.

The two women started back in fear the moment they saw Tasunke Paytah's grey face with spittle caked at the sides of his mouth. Two of the men, Ed and Takota, had hoisted him up between them with his arms around their shoulders. Another younger man led with a lantern. They dragged Tasunka Paytah into the back room and lifted him onto the overstuffed sofa where he lay with one arm askew over his head, the other hanging limply off the side. Hantaywee, wailing with grief, sat down on the heavy arm chair and rocked back and forth, still holding the candle as she stared straight ahead. Anpaytoo rushed to her brother's side, and sat on the floor next to the couch, taking his hand in hers.

The three men conferred before the two strangers left. Takota sat down in the kitchen, unable to speak. Anpaytoo stood, walked over and placed her strong hands on her mother's sturdy shoulders, trying to comfort her with a massage. Hantaywee's eyes were filling with tears that dripped down her sallow cheeks while her throat choked her wails into silence. *Where was her big, strong, handsome, strapping Tasunke Paytah,* she thought, *who fought the spotted fever with such vigor? She remembered his long strides when he ran around the tipis of their settlement, his black hair streaming in the wind, as if he were a fiery pony.*

When Takota heard her muffled sobs, he approached her and coaxed her to come with him and sit on the floor in front of the overstuffed chair, which served as their backrest. He took the candle from her and placed it on the floor in front of them where it glimmered like a receding campfire. Gently he embraced her, and they leaned against each other, falling asleep in each other's arms while Anpaytoo returned to sit beside her brother and to rest her head on the side of the sofa where Paytah slept.

At daybreak, she awoke to the smell of coffee and flapjacks cooking on the fry pan, and she arose to peek around the corner into the kitchen where she saw Hantaywee, ladling out their breakfast. While Anyapaytoo sat down at the kitchen table for the meal, Takota entered from the back room to intercept old man Casmir Wojcik who was tramping down the pathway to the house at a furious pace. He met with Takota at the doorway, face to face.

"The best housekeeper I ever had, and she hasn't shown up. Why?" He blustered and gestured at Anpaytoo.

Takota took him aside onto the porch. After a few moments of conversation, Casmir reappeared at the doorway, wringing his hands. "Oh *dziewcyna*! How could they! And now your brother..." He turned to Takota and murmured, "Remember what I said." and stormed down the path, muttering under his breath.

Anpaytoo resumed sitting on the floor beside her brother while he lay, half conscious, on the sofa. He grinned at her, his head propped upon the pillows on the arm rest, his hand on his stomach where he felt excruciating pain.

"We're in a fine mess," he said, his deep voice wavering.

"That we are, but we'll survive, " she answered with resolution to give him courage.

"We always have." He raised himself up on his arm, and his eyes had a faint gleam in them. "We almost drove the white men out of here, did you know that? We won every battle, until their troops came with their canons."

"They were fighting their own war against themselves."

He smirked. "Fighting against owning people while they're trying to own us? We would rather die."

"They rob us of our territories instead."

"And they'll keep on stealing from us until the last one of us is killed. Then they'll make up stories about us like that Longfellow guy did with his character, Hiawatha. Imagine that, an Iroquis wandering around here in Minnesota!"

Anpaytoo laughed. "Well, they say that he was carrying on with Minnehaha. They even named a place of falling waters after her, she who never existed."

They remained silent for awhile.

"Do you think that if we retreat to Grandmother's Land (Canada) and return again, we ever will reclaim what we lost?" Anpaytoo asked.

Paytah lay back, exhausted, speaking in a hoarse voice. "That's hoping for too much. How can we get the forests back that they destroyed by building their wooden boxes of houses and stores and factories? It took many years for those trees to grow. I thought maybe I could get some payment for their theft of our trees, but I was only fooling myself. It was such a stupid idea – getting even that way. I let crazy people drive me crazy."

"Well, it wasn't such a bad idea. At least you got back something of what they owe us." She stroked his arm, hoping he would combat the illness that was wasting his powers.

"They agreed to pay us for our land. Instead, they took the land and sent their cannons and troops. What kind of people do that?"

Anpaytoo slid her hand in his and he clasped it. "They don't even know how to live well with each other," she said.

He nodded. "We heard reports about that war they were fighting with brothers killing brothers – thousands were maimed and killed — over property rights to the black slaves they shipped here from Africa. They want to own everything when you can't really own anything."

Anpaytoo nodded. "Chief Little Crow warned us."

"But we had no choice. Little Crow agreed to three treaties – each time they took more and more land from us; each time they gave the money owed us to the traders instead of us. Well, we beat them at Little Big Horn." He smiled with satisfaction, and said in response to Anpaytoo's surpised look, "We pitched our best, Crazy Horse, and their best, Custer, against each other and we won; after that, there's no way they can say they are better than us."

"Takota says that we outnumbered them," said Anpaytoo softly, realizing that Tasunke Paytah must have overheard reports from the white men at the mills.

"Yeah, that's what the wisa'chu say; they were so worked up, they wouldn't stop talking about it. But the army tried to surprise us – in broad daylight. What wisa'chu's army fights us without hiding in the darkness of dawn or dusk?" Tasuke Paytah shook his head. "You know where we are strong, where they aren't?"

She looked up at his face, which seemed to reveal an inner radiance.

"We are strong with the spirit of Sitting Bull; that's where, and it scares the hell outta the white man..." He leaned back into the pillows and nodded his head. "Yes, our spirits will haunt them with the spirit of the medicine man-warrior Sitting Bull, who will walk with us. Their cannons will not be able to drive away our spirits. The invaders have no red road to follow, like we have, a road that makes us strong against every evil thing."

"Remember, Paytah, when we roamed the forests? When we gathered the roots, herbs, berries in a place, alive with birds, rabbits, raccoons, beaver, foxes, wolves, deer, bears and coyotes? When we swam in the rivers, many fish would come up to greet us in the clear water?"

"We belonged to mother earth and to each other." He sighed. "We had so much then. Even though we had to work hard for it, we didn't want for anything. Everything was plentiful in this land of ours. Now we are near starving. We have to buy food from the wasi'chus who think they own everything."

"Takota says that we can live well in Canada. The white man hasn't settled there."

"Hah! The English and French live there. Maybe not so many, but it will be the same. They will drive us away, as far as they can and then corner us, like the U.S. troops did at Wood Lake." He became pensive while he thought about the Minnesota battle, one that he had only heard of as a child, listening to accounts around the tribal campfire. "Aii!" He cried out. "And there were traitors among us, or so it is said."

"Let's take our chances on Grandmother's Land (Canada) even though we never forget the lakes and streams, hills and valleys here." Anpaytoo tried to calm him, rubbing his arm.

"I would rather die here." He began closing his eyes. "I drank water at the shop, and it has poisoned me." His eyes flew open briefly. "Leaps Up was my dog, you know. Let him be with me. That would make me glad." He began murmuring a delirious prayer of death.

She shook her head, and shuddered. "No. Don't think that way." She leaned over and whispered, "You're strong. You can get better. Hantaywee will heal you with herbs and teas. And then you must come with us to live freely as we did before. I would give the whole forest for you Tasunka Paytah. They can have it. Just let me have you alive and with us." Tears flooded her eyes and flowed down her cheeks as she choked on other thoughts she wanted to say to comfort him.

But he had drifted off to sleep. Hantaywee came from the shadows of the room and touched him. "His fever has broken," she said and found a blanket to cover him.

"That's good, isn't it?" Anpaytoo asked.

"We can only hope so,. Come daughter, and help me harvest the garden."

With a look of expectation, Anpaytoo followed Hantaywee. They proceeded to harvest the peas, pole beans, tomatoes, potatoes and squash. They decided not to strip the stand of corn until the cobs had ripened. While Anpaytoo cut and gathered the vegetables, slipping them into a muslin bag, tied to her waist, she felt enclosed in the abundance burgeoning from the earth. The land would never forsake us, she thought. It would always provide as it had when she, Tasunka Paytah and Tokala Kohana played together in their village. Bending over her task, she became lost in the memories of their adventures with the crickets, grasshoppers and fireflies and the geese and ducks that were constantly present, pecking at fallen grain. *My brothers! My brothers! She thought. The future held the same fruitful promise,* she thought, *when her two brothers, their parents, and she were reunited with Chayton Enapay and his clan.*

She looked up to see her father on the river bank and walked upt to him to admire his catch of fish. Takota appeared to be lost in thought. Having climbed up the knoll from ferrying some travelers across the Mississippi, he carried a string of fish that he had caught after dropping off the group with their team of horses and wagons onto the west bank. The sharp bite in the wind left him with a look of apprehension. He was hoping that winter would arrive late this year, so that they would have time to make it to Canada before the storms that awaited them. The sharp breeze from the north told him differently, that they were in for an early and long, frigid haul He recalled the icy winters when they were grateful for the warm shelter of Jon Griswald's cabin. Maybe they would have to stay until next spring. He did not look forward to that.

Hantaywee, glanced up, smiled at him, and carried her bag of vegetables to the porch where she deposited them before she slipped into the house to begin dinner and to look in on Tasunka Paytah. She disappeared inside for but a few moments when her cry reverberated into the very bones of Anpaytoo, who rushed into the house with Takota, who dropped his fish on the porch, as he ran to Hantaywee's side where she knelt beside Paytah whose face had turned ashen, frozen in the grip of death, and yet peaceful in the last sleep he'd had with them.

Hantaywee and Anpaytoo wailed and sheared off their long hair. Takota sang the death song, his face twisted in anguish as he cut away each of his braids and then, he passed his hand over, closing the eyes of his son, now lying cold and lifeless before him. Through the long night, they cleansed the body. Takota dressed Tasunke Paytah in his finest, and cut off a lock of his son's hair wrapping it in a piece of buffalo hide for his sacred bundle. Hantaywee brought forth some sage, lit it in a bowl, and she waved its fragrance throughout the room. Anpaytoo sat motionless and numb beside her brother who had crossed into the spirit world too soon. With her mother, she, too, had ragged hair around her face, which was contorted in agony, for they had hoped to have him beside them on the long, harrowing trip north. They had wanted to talk about his life when he was away from them and then their ongoing expectations. But the years behind and before them remained unexplored, an empty gap that would never be filled. Silent as he was now and forever, they remained disconsolate as the family sat around the glowing bowl of sage throughout the night.

At daybreak, Takota left his grieving wife and daughter while he headed toward old man Casmir's, who had told him to ask him for anything, anything at all. Takota returned with Casmir's horse and wagon, a fitting funeral carriage to transport his son to a sacred grounds up river, which was similar to burial places where the Dakota had enshrined their dead for hundreds of years.

Hantaywee swaddled Paytah in their finest blankets and buffalo robes, and the three of them lifted him onto the back of the wagon next to Leaps Up rolled into another red and yellow blanket and placed in the corner where he lay in a red-golden heap. Hantaywee climbed up front, clutching the sacred bundle they had made from Tasunk Paytah's hair and favorite things, while Takota added some shovels and posts in the back and Anpaytoo climbed on carrying a basket of food, herbs and wildflowers. With Takota and Hantaywee on the front driver's seat and Anpaytoo sitting behind them next to Tasunka Paytah, the family headed upstream; Casmir's roan jogged ahead at a steady pace.

22

STALKED BY DEATH

Arriving at midday, Takota realized how far he had strayed from the ways of the old Dakota village, which left not a trace of its former existence. Though they were on the outskirts of the town, land was being cleared for more white settlers which Takota felt was much too close to where they had once lived. *'Who gave them the right to drive us away like that?' he thought, looking around at what had once been a Dakota community. Only two birchbark trees by the lakeside marked where they had once had their settlement.*

When they reached the sacred funeral grounds they called for Wicasa. "Who goes there?" A gruff voice emerged from the darkness. Startled, Takota saw the figure, standing in the dusk, the buffalo horns gleaming on his skull cap. A long necklace of bears' teeth hung down his chest, his face, painted red on one side and black on the other; his fringed buckskin breeches swayed and swished with his regalia. He appeared ghostly indeed, and the shadows of the stand of what was left of the trees were an eerie accompaniment to his exotic appearance.

Wicasa and Takota approached and grasped each others' shoulders. "I still guard the sacred ancestor's grounds, but it has not been well for us here," Wicasa said as he stepped back and glanced at the area where the white men were encroaching. "They think this place is haunted. To make them sure of this, I shoot arrows at them and leave markings on the trees, scattering beads here and there. I make a good owl hoot too, and my night chanting must keep them awake at night."

Wicasa approached Hantaywee and Anpaytoo, showing concern through the deep set eyes in his painted face "You are coming here too often. It is not good when death stalks you."

Takota walked beside him and placed his hand on Wicasa's shoulder. "My friend, we have lost a son," he said. At that, Wicasa, stood back and looked up at the enveloping clouds and cried out to Wakan Tanka, a cry that echoed throughout the area, resounding against the trees to the very skies above, a grating tenor voice leaving an indelible impression on those who heard it.

After his prayer in which he addressed all that was wakan (sacred), Hantaywee and Anpaytoo jumped off the wagon, and the group used their strength to shovel holes in the ground where they dropped the four posts that Tacota had brought with them from a supply of logs left over from building the cabin. He had hewn forks on the upward ends, as he had done, hastily for "Troubled Spirit." It was as if wooden arms were beseeching the spirits in the heavens above, like the many other wooden arms surrounding them, where vultures perched, waiting. Together, the family lashed more poles lengthwise across the forks and covered them with willow and ash brush, making a soft bed where they planned to heft up and place the bodies of Tasunke Paytah and his little dog, Leaps Up.

"Óh wait," said Hantaywee who sat down and held her head in her hands while she wept.

After they lifted her, trembling, to her feet and let her recover while sitting under a tree, they worked on until they finished at sunset, which sent a warm, mellow light through the trees and softly on their shoulders. Tasunke Paytah was heavy, and Takota had slipped a little when he cimbed up with his son on his shoulders to lay him on the scaffold bed. Wicasa stood below to steady them on the structure. Hantaywee and Anpaytoo climbed part way to help. As they drew closer, Hantaywee with muffled sobs sprinkled sacred tobacco over her son. Anpaytoo arranged corn, potatoes, dried berries and pemmican on the scaffold and around the colorfully wrapped Leaps Up next to him. All the while they sang the death dirge, wishing him a safe journey home, and then jumped down into a circle dance. Finally, they stood back and gazed at the scaffold, which was about seven feet above the ground. For their brave Tasunke Paytah they had opened the gates of the pathway to the stars; the journey there would lead him home. In the face of these lofty ideals, they, themselves, were a bedraggled tiospaye, in ragged clothes and with their hair chopped off, made even more disheveled by the whirling wind.

While Wicasa chanted a Tsamsiuwahkan (ceremonial song), he approached the scaffold and scattered tobacco around it, his thin, drawn face, silhouetted in the fading light. Holding his sacred pipe befor him he held it up in six directions, each with a separate incantation to the spirits that dwelled there. Again and again the party sang the death song of the thirty-eight braves at their execution, for they felt that Tasunke Paytah would not have died if their tribe had been allowed to live in their Minnesota homeland.

When they were finished, Hantaywee moaned and cried out, "My fist born boy! My brave, strong Tasunke Paytah"

Wicasa turned to them. "You may join me at my hut. It's not much, but we must have a ceremonial feast for a son." And so they brought a few items to Wicasa's and he treated them to the traditional meal. All the while, Hantaywee could not stop rocking and weeping.

"You can stay here and mourn for awhile," Wicasa insisted over the firelight while the moon disappeared behind clouds. "Tasunke Paytah was your first born son; that is a hard blow. You need to ease it with much song and circle dancing.

"No, my friend." Takota leaned forward and held Wicasa's arm. "The old man who let us use his horse and wagon needs them to travel to his workplace in the morning. And we must return before the white man sees us gone and takes our cabin. We need to winter there before we join Tokala Kohana and Chayton Enapay in Canada,"

Like the humming of wings came her voice. "I remember your mother, Wicasa."

She was so sweet to me, teaching me how to be a Wisdom Keeper. How I wish she were here with me." Hantaywee spoke in a gentle undertone. "She taught me how to plant, harvest and grind the corn and prepare the deer meat and the deer skin. My mother and the women of the camp were so helpful to me. They guided me since I was very young into the *Ta Awi Cha Lowan*. And now my daughter is becoming a woman..." Her voice caught, and Anpaytoo put her arm around her mother who grew plaintive. "We are so alone, Wicasa. Without the others, we have no medicine men or wisdom keepers to guide us. We no longer seem to have the strength to go on. What is happening to us Wicasa? Are we to become ghost people?"

"The white man thinks we are" Wicasa said softly while bending toward her. "But he's in for a big surprise. We don't become ghosts so easily." After the tiospaye of Takota Wachinskowa promised to keep the sacred bundle of Tasunke Paytah's hair, Wicasa took it and held it over the fire, praying.

For the first time in a long while, Hantaywee's face softened. "Yes, let's surprise them,' she murmured and chanted a death song for Tasunke Paytah.

"Sleep sun

Take my first born boy

With you

Rise moon

Guide him

Along the good way

Let us meet again someday

Where Wakan Tanka lives."

Wicasa whispered to Hantaywee, "You can tell your daughter all you know about how she can live in the good way, and how she can raise her children in a good way. You can be her holy woman. Give her what you remember. These are hard times, when we are separated from one another like this. I pray to Wankan Tanka that it will not last nor be for long."

Takota put his hand on Wicasa's shoulder again. "They will not have seen the last of us, not as long as mother earth gives us life. But we must go now; it's a long night's journey back. We will visit each other again."

Wicasa approached Anpaytoo. "I know that you are full of sorrow now, but Wankan Tanka still wants you to know how sacred you are during these times in your young life. We cannot honor you today for it takes much preparation. You will need your own tipi that I will build for you and then, after the ceremony, you must spend time in the Inipi (Sweat) Lodge over there to be purified before you return to live with the others.

I will collect the buffalo skull, wild cherries, the wooden cup, the sacred pipe, Ree tobacco, kinnikinnik, a knife, a stone hatchet, sweet grass and sage. With these things we will show you how to be like Mother Earth, for yours will be the most sacred fruits of all, your children, you will raise in a sacred manner. So, you see, this ceremony would take days, which we do not have right now." He bowed his head and purified his pipe, chanting with it in four directions and sending its smoke over her to honor her.

As they departed, a full, harvest moon lighted their way. Hantaywee huddled next to Takota in the driver's seat while Anpaytoo sat in the wagon with her back to them, trying to hide her tears that would not stop flowing.

23

CHANGE OF PLANS

Takota had found a bag of money on the table when they returned from the Dakota cemetary. It was Anpaytoo's last payment from old man Casmir, and they still had money they had saved. Bending to the task before them, they harvested the entire garden, after which they stored their crops in bins and Takota hunted whatever game was left, mostly rabbits. They made ready for a long, treacherous winter, for, as Takota had dreaded, an early frost set upon them with its fierce freezing winds that moaned through the surrounding break of oaks. Ice crept up the river and hemmed in the ferry boat. They could expect no more business there. Rumors reached them that the city planners were designing a bridge to be built downstream to span the great river. We will be gone from here by then, thought Takota with a grim set to his mouth.

"Come inside, woman," Takota would say while shoving wood in the kitchen stove with his strong hands, keeping the fires strong. But Hantaywee would sit outside, shriveled like a straw doll, in the most wretched weather, wrapped in a red woolen blanket, singing softly to herself and rocking on the front porch chair. She sang about going home, dancing around the fires again, and she'd beat on her knees as if they were drums. "Come inside, Hantaywee," Takota would say, his voice disappearing in the winds, while clasping her hands in his and pulling her up, making her lean on him while he wrapped the blanket more tightly around her and guided her into the kitchen and seated her in front of the stove.

"I cannot wait anymore," she would say and rest her head on her hand. "Oh my Tasunke Paytah!" The color had drained out of her face which had turned sallow with grief.

"It was good that we were here for him when he left for the spirit world, and that we were able give him a decent ceremony," Takota said while trying to comfort her. "He went with dignity, something the white men would have never given him."

"But must we wait forever?" Her plaintive voice rose against the wind.

"As long as the snow falls and the winds whip it into a frenzy, we cannot leave – unless you want to die out there, trying to get to your other son."

"Dying out there, in here, what's the difference?" Her desultory body, clad in buckskin, slumped in a chair.

Anpaytoo realized that she had to pick up the slack in the family chores. She cooked and cleaned while Hantaywee continued with her erratic routine, barely eating and wandering about the house during the blizzards that wracked it, seeking the peace that never came. Her thin, drawn face revealed her inner agony, the lines across her forehead, deepened, the hollows in her cheeks, darkened, her eyes constricted with pain, her lips, a thin, tight, blue line. At times, she whispered Tasunke Paytah's name and enumerated his qualities, as if she were meditating on a string of beads. Often, she could be seen seated on the sofa where he had lain, her hands pressed upon her heart. If Anpaytoo drew close enough, she could hear her mother muttering, "If they had never come, we could have had a good life here. Why, Wakan Tanka, did you set them loose upon us and our Mother Earth? Why?"

They changed their sleeping arrangements in which Anpaytoo slept in the small back bedroom under a buffalo robe in order to be close to the fireplace in the parlor where Paytah had last rested so long ago before he worked for the mill. Takota and Hantaywee lay in the large bedroom under the quilts where her husband held her close, trying to keep her from wandering off in the night. She would slip away at dawn, and he would find her, standing in the middle of the front pathway, holding her hands out to catch the snowfall.

Whispering, "Tasunke Paytah," she would laugh with an eerie sigh. "I know you are here. Why are you hiding behind the snowflakes? Why did you stumble up this path with the others holding you? Where have you gone? Don't leave us forever."

Takota would throw a blanket around her and gently lead her back into the house where he rubbed her cold hands and feet and sat with her before the warm fire in the kitchen stove. Anpaytoo awoke and found them huddled together there where she served them oatmeal with honey that they had stored in jars in the cupboards behind her. The simple meal filled their mouths with sweet warmth while the winter winds whistled and knocked at the windows, like a stranger seeking entrance. All the while, the chill of the season was dispelled by the thoughts they shared with one another.

24

SIGNS OF A NEW BEGINNING

"You know, they have taken everything from us," said Takota, "but one thing." He would rub his chin under a faint smirk.

Anpaytoo smiled for she knew what that was and she joined in with him. "They cannot take away our spirit. It will live forever on this land." She said in unison with him.

"Already the names of the nations and our spoken words are everywhere – the Delaware, the Illinois, the Massachusetts, the Dakotas, the Utes, the Alabamas," he said. "Do you think that's by accident?" he asked them "No, our ancestors are telling us that they are still here, and that as long as the earth survives, we will survive with it."

"Maybe that's why the white man is destroying the earth," said Hantaywee in a cracked voice. "He wants to destroy us, too."

"We won't let them," Takota said gruffly, placing down his cup of herb tea.

"Hah! Old man, how can you say that? Look what they did to our son. And the rest of us have been driven away. Why must we flee to Canada when this is our land? Our children were born and raised here, Takota. It's our home. Yet, we're letting them drive us away."

"We will always fight back — together our spirits will survive; together we will win again. Wakan Tanka will surprise us as he did at Little Big Horn." Takota arose and put on his hunting gear.

He continued to hunt rabbits and set up an ice fishing hut on the river while Anpaytoo kept Hantaywee company. They tried to stay within the confines of the house because whenever she and Hantaywee walked to the store to buy necessities, the town folk would glare at them and the shop keeper would treat them with rude disdain. They would gather their cloaks around themselves and hasten home, while the crowd milled around them, like a rumbling storm cloud about to break. It was on one of these excursions that Anpaytoo told Hantaywee about Zeke.

"Aii, my daughter, my light that appears in the darkness," Hantaywee moaned, her face contorted with anxiety. She turned to look longingly at Anpaytoo, brushed back hair from her cheeks, and held her close. "How can we protect you? They would trample on you, too, as they do the flowers in the fields. Aii And you are just entering into your womanhood, you are just beginning to become part of the great mystery of the moon and tides and seasons. We must beg Wankan Tanka not to let you be taken…" Her voice trailed off. Then Hantawee realized that though she was bearing an unbearable burden, the knowledge that her daughter needed her more than ever seemed to have awakened in her an awareness of the life around her. She looked at her daughter and realized that she was needed in this life, not in the one beyond where Tasunke Paytah had gone.

That night, she gazed up at the sky and its trail of the spirits (*Wanaghi Tachanku)* that the white man called the Milky Way, and she meditated on Tasunke Paytah running with the stars and past the old woman who sends spirits either to their eternal fall in the universe or sends them to the dwelling place with Wanka Tanka. "Let him pass," she prayed. "Let him run to his heavenly home. He was good, generous, strong and brave. A mother couldn't have asked for a better son," she beseeched in prayer, hoping that the old woman heard her and waved him on. At that moment, she saw a star glimmer brightly among the others, and she took that as a sign that he had arrived.

When the dawn broke, sparkling on the massive silver ice flow, Takota awoke, and realized that Hantaywee was off on one of her romps again. He found her standing in the middle of the icy river, holding a deer with legs splayed; the animal was slipping and sliding in an attempt to get across.

"What are you doing, woman?" he yelled.

"I'm becoming a better hunter than you," she yelled back and laughed, a clear laugh that echoed in the frozen air liked struck crystal. "Come, help me." Breathing heavily but with a joy in the puff of each breath, she proceeded to drag the struggling deer across with her. At that moment Takota knew that she was no longer lost in the mournful outskirts of the spirit world, seeking her son. She had returned to the land of the living and was rejoicing in it.

He joined her, pulling the heavy resisting load, for the deer twisted and turned as it fought for its life. Takota made swift work of killing the animal once they reached the shoreline where he hung it outside and dressed it down next to the shed. He stood back and examined his work.

Giving thanks to the deer and Wakan Tanka, he cried out, "at last, we will have venison,"

"And clothing and moccasins," Anpaytoo added, having stepped outside, to admire their catch. The icy wind whipped her loose hair about and lifted the blanket she had wrapped around her. She had exchanged her thin calico and leather shoes for a buckskin dress and fur lined moccasins. "What a generous gift is the deer from Wakan Tanka." She reached out to feel the deer's rough winter coat and stepped back to watch it swing in the wind.

When the sun seemed farthest away and yet poised to return at a time that the white settlers called Christmas, the tiospaye of Takota feasted on the newly caught venison with cornmeal bread, and dried berries that they had stored. It seemed to be a turning point, one in which the movement of the sun toward them signified a new beginning. The small group circle danced on the shore around a bonfire, bright enough to glimmer in the river ice like waves undulating in the twilight. Takota recalled the grandiose feasts they once had during those days of expectations. He remembered his father showing him how the sun moved away, almost as if the earth had lost it, and then began returning after they had celebrated its retreat, knowing that at that moment it would return to guide them through the harsh winter months ahead.

Anpaytoo danced, letting the winds send their icy fingers through the strands of her hair, flowing black in the dusk. She noticed how her old parent's cheeks bloomed rosy rubbed by the touch of the powers of the North and how cleansed and invigorated they all felt. The sun will return, she thought, as will her brothers, one, Tasunke Paytah, would always be with them, his spirit hovered nearby and probably even celebrated. She longed to see him again with his tall, strong body, bent back as he looked skyward, and he would call like an alpha wolf to Wakan Tanka once gain. The other, Tokala Kohana, who wandered somewhere else on Turtle Island, would return to guide them back to the tribe's quarters up North. She felt sure of that, even though she bore the emptiness, the sharp pain that accompanied the loss of his presence.

The full moon was moving in and out among the clouds that night as it accompanied them back to their cabin. Hantaywee thought again about Anpaytoo's newly emerging womanhood. *I will do all that I can,* she thought and fervently hoped that the winter would be a short one, so that they could soon take their journey northward. *Anypaytoo needs the tribe,* she thought. *We all need each other.*

25

THE INTERLOPERS

Voices and fists banged as if someone were pounding on her head with a pick ax, but it was at the door. Anpaytoo awoke with a start, sat up, and out of bed. She ran toward the parlor sofa where she stopped and pressed her fingers against her temples, shivering in the icy cold, sliced through by the sounds of the door that crashed open allowing three dark, heavy figures to stand in the white morning fog at the doorway of the room.

Someone else was pounding, nailing something to the front of the house.

"You, get out!"

She recognized Zeke's voice and watched his wiry frame uncoil toward the bedroom where Hantaywee and Takota were aroused, but not ready for the rough hands that dragged them out of their room.

"You don't belong here, you dirty redskins!" He pushed and shoved the couple toward the door. "That piece of shit half breed of yours killed two federal agents."

Anpaytoo managed to pull on her moccasins and wrap a blanket around her as she brushed past Zeke and ran, slipping on the ice-covered walkway, and, yet, she made her way across the street to old man Casmir's. Her breath was coming in short pants while she pounded on the door and shouted.

"Help! Please help! They're throwing us out – those men and your son." Casmir, half awake and in his night shirt, opened the door and peered past her at the scene on the street. He pulled back.

"I'm afraid I can't help you," he said, looking at her through the sad drowsiness of his round eyes. "They're following orders from the federal government. No Sioux are allowed in Minnesota – ever since the uprising was put down." He shook his head, then looked past her. "Why they're barefoot and uncovered."

"And what about our things? Our supplies for the winter? You can't just throw us out like this We will surely die," Anpayto insisted with a firmness in her voice.

"Your supplies? Ah! I think you may have something there." He left, but after a few moments, he returned fully dressed and he and Anpaytoo walked over to confront the four men who surrounded the evicted family. While Anpaytoo rushed into the house to retrieve blankets and moccasins for Takota and Hantaywee, Casmir struck a deal with the group.

After the men left with Zeke, his eyes gleaming like those of a hungry coyote, Takota's family made ready to leave. Casmir explained the agreement to Anpaytoo while he helped load his wagon with their supplies for the long trip to Wicasa's. He had told the men that Anpaytoo, the one he called Anya, was his Polish housekeeper on loan to the Indians, so she was to continue to stay with him, but that the Indians had purchased goods with legal tender and so those goods were legally theirs. He had promised the men that he'd have the Indians out and gone with all of their goods before noon, pointing out that they were lucky it was Sunday and no one had to work. Anpaytoo helped lift the supplies onto the wagon, but her heart was heavy with dread when she sat down among their things in the back, holding the sacred bundle of Tasunke Paytah close to her heart, while Takota and Hantaywee were hunkered down on the front driver's seat, next to Casmir, whose red roan, jogged along the worn path northward to where Tasunke Paytah lay buried.

Legal tender, she thought, *was more important than her mother's and father's lives. And what were they going to do with her? Did Casmir now own her?* She shuddered at the thought of his ownership of her as his full time 'Polish housekeeper.'.

The barren trees swayed like a whispering chorus in the wind, moaning along the trail. Theirs seemed like a funeral march to mourn the remnants of a village that once was vibrant with the life emerging from the toil that kept it going. Anpaytoo wrapped her blanket tightly around her while she held the sacred bundle. Dressed in buckskin as she was, she recalled Wicasa's sad warning, "It is not good when death stalks you like this." And the spectral trees seemed to be saying just that. Were the trees accusing them of not protecting them enough? Too many of them had been felled while the family stood helpless before the onslaught. There were trees she had known, the sturdy oaks with their wide leaves, the red maples and the silvery white birches – trees and bushes that they had used to mark their way when they went hunting or foraging for roots and berries – were gone. Along the way to their old settlement, houses were sprouting up like large clumps of weeds in the fields where there once was a dense undergrowth in the forests.

Takota had told her stories about the fires that he had helped set and control when he was a young man. "They spread throughout the underbrush," he said, waving his spread hands out over the brush in the forest. "That's how we cleared it during the Moons of the Falling Leaves, after which, the forest was dampened down by the snowfalls. At the same time, we had a good hunting season when many four leggeds ran away from the flames. We stocked up for the Moons of the Popping Trees (December) all the way up until the end of the Moon of the Snowblind (March). Then during the Moon of the Red Grass Appearing (April) we saw hungry bears on the prowl. We had made the earth ready for the growing grass, plants, and berries that were able to get a good start with all the room we gave them. Back then," he reminisced, "we could ride four across through wide paths we had made in the forest. And Wankan Tanka rewarded us with an abundance of food and furs so that we never wanted for anything."

Anpaytoo nodded off, remembering her childhood in the vast, park-like surroundings, which were disrupted by the invaders. After the war that had broken out in Minnesota when she was only ten winters old, she saw warriors with rags tied around their wounds stagger into the camp, accompanied by distraught women and wretched children. They wandered into the settlement, day and night, with dirty, blood-splattered faces and ragged blankets wrapped around their thin bodies. Her earliest memories were of the members of her tribe who welcomed them and shared their food, clothing and lodgings with the refugees and even built more tipis for them. While seated around the campfire in his large tipi, Chief Kangee spoke about how honored we were to include "our relatives," the travelers, in our lives. Everyone participated, even little Anpaytoo when Hantaywee showed her how to apply herbed poultices to their injuries. She recalled the warmth she had felt while growing up in the midst of such kindness which softened the murmurs about the atrocity. "Thirty eight hanged" the newcomers had said, shaking their heads, enumerating the never to be forgotten names of their tribal members. They mourned their beloveds' burial in a mass grave, where the wasi'chus felt free to desecrate the bodies. Then came even worse news during the Moon when the Ponies Shed (May).

"Father Lincoln from Washington has issued a decree which declares that all Sioux must leave the state of Minnesota immediately," Takota had cried out before he stopped and stooped over, his hands on his knees, for he was breathless from running. The horse he was riding had dropped a few miles back. "I tell you this," he said, standing straight, glistening with sweat, "for the State of Minnesota has put a bounty on our heads."

The women wailed and the braves shouted out until Chief Kangee stepped in and lifted his hand for silence. "How can this be?" he asked in his hoarse voice. "We are friendly Indians and never once did battle with the white man."

"It's true, I tell you," Takota had cried out. "The white settlers are shooting us on sight. Chief Little Crow was shot to death in a field. His son, who escaped, can tell you." Takota walked away to his tipi and into the arms of Hantaywee while Anpaytoo had cried in utter confusion. For years afterward, Hantaywee patiently talked to Anpaytoo about the traumatic events around them. So despite all that she had seen, embraced by the community, she felt safe. How she longed for that feeling again. She realized how much she needed the Dakota tribe and the wisdom of the old ways.

Suddenly, Casmir pulled on the reins and halted the wagon. "We'll go no further," he declared, climbing down from his seat when they reached the burial grounds. He unloaded the wagon, heaving the goods on the snowy ground. Anpaytoo was shocked out of her revery.

"But, we need to find Wicasa's place where they can stay," Anpaytoo leapt off, rushed over and pleaded with him.

"We'll go no further," Casmir repeated, dropping a chest on the ground and glaring at her. "This place is haunted, and I won't stay here any longer than I have to."

"It's all right, Anpaytoo," Takota muttered, taking her aside. "We know where Wicasa lives." Hantaywee stood beside him, shivering while clutching a blanket around her and standing in the bitter windswept clearing."Our tipis weren't far from here," she said. "Do you remember?"

Anpaytoo nodded and looked toward the two silver birches that marked the village entry and then she gazed off in the distance toward Tasunke Paytah's grave. "We were always close to those in the spirit world," she said then turned toward her parents. "How will you survive in Wicasa's small place? Oh tell me that he's here, that you will find him and live."

Hantaywee tightened her blanket with one hand and with the other, held Anpaytoo's hand. "Old man Casmir, there, told us that he has bolted the doors and changed the locks to keep his son out of his house, and that his son's wife does the laundry now. She picks it up and returns it. If you make friends with her, you will be safe," she assured her while she held her hands in a vice grip and pulled her toward her. "Anpaytoo, you must live. Do you understand?" She caught her daughter's frightened gaze in her steadfast one. "No matter what happens, you must live — for us. When the snows clear, during the Moon When the Ponies Shed, we will come back for you. Know this — we will never abandon you, for you are part of the circle of hope, the sacred hoop and the stone wheel. Do you understand? Don't ever forget that." Hantaywee and her daughter held each other in a tight embrace. "After a few moons, we will go on to Canada together," her mother continued, kissing her daughter on the forehead before they parted.

But I am not Polish, she thought with a grimace. *How can old man Casmir pass* me off *as Polish?* The men he told hadn't argued with him; they seemed relieved to have resolved any problems without having to involve government authorities. She wrapped extra blankets around both her parents for they looked so fragile, standing in the whirling snow, surrounded by their meager belongings. She did not want to let go of them, but Casmir was calling and had already turned the roan and wagon around. She walked backwards so that she could look at her parents and, finally, climbed up onto the seat next to Casmir while he clicked the reins on the roan's sturdy flanks. Anpaytoo turned to watch her mother and father grow smaller in the distance, like a nest of whippoorwills surrounded by the white, grey ground. All the while, she thought she saw the shadow of a tall figure, lurking among the trees; she was sure it was Wicasa,

26

CAPTIVITY

The maid's quarters, situated on the ground floor off the living room and not far from the adjacent dining room and kitchen, were not all that unpleasant. After Casmir showed her the room, he wandered off into the kitchen to boil water for tea. She closed the door behind her. The dark, polished mahogany headboard stood out in contrast to the double bed with its pillows and blankets under a white crocheted coverlet. At the foot of the bedstead and against the wall was a matching vanity where she sat down on its chair to stare at her bedraggled image in the mirror. Her hair hung in ragged disarray around her wind burned face, dirty and stained with tears. But the almond eyes, high cheek bones and full lips had a stunning luminosity of their own.

Slowly she arose, turned, unwrapped and laid out her scant wardrobe on the bed, which consisted of one calico and one gingham dress, a pair of stockings, leather shoes and the required underwear. Rubbing her hands on her buckskin dress, she felt its smooth, sturdy surface, water proof and wind proof; she was as reluctant to remove it as she was to part with her warm moccasins. She examined their bead and quill work, touching the zig zag lightening patterns and rays of the sun. As she looked up, she saw that in the corner stood an upright, mahogany dresser, which she approached to pull open a drawer, where she folded and stuffed the dresses.

Feeling desolate, she began her long siege when she climbed under the covers of the bed and lay there in a deathlike slumber.

"Dziewcyna! Dziewcyna!" Someone was shaking her, lifting her out of the wind and the rains where she had wandered, crying out for Hantaywee, Takota, Tasunke Paytah, and Tokala Kohana. She could feel Leaps Up at her side, eagerly sniffing the ground. She stumbled, and then crawled on the snowy ground, her hands and face frozen. Reaching out with one hand, like a blind girl, she whimpered, "Where am I? What am I doing here? Hantaywee! Mama!"

"Dziewcyna!"(little girl) Casmir was wiping her face with a cold wet cloth. "It's been two days now, and you haven't eaten. Dziewcyna!" He held her head up and tried to force a spoonful of soup into her mouth. The soup dribbled out the sides and down her chin. He placed the bowl on the end table and stood up. "I will have to call the nuthouse, and they will take you away forever. Do you want that? Then you will never see your mama and poppa again."

"Never see them again?" she said in a weak voice as she groped at the covers and stared at Casmir, at his rotund face with the furrowed brows over his bushy eyebrows.

"Look." He sat down next to her. "You will see them in the spring."

"How many moons?" Her thin, fagile voice floated across the room.

"Moons?"

She grimaced through cracked lips. "Months."

"Oh, I'd say, two, three at the most depending on the weather." He picked up the bowl of soup again, lifted her head, and began spooning the liquid into her mouth. She stopped him, sat up, took the bowl, hungrily finished and felt warmed and strengthen as if by good medicine.

"How old are you, Dziewcyna? Takota told me about fourteen, fifteen winters."

"Years, winters mean years." She sat up and pushed away the covers. "I can return to them, and we three can leave together like we planned?" Her voice was slurred.

"You have my word on it." His voice was almost a whisper. "Meanwhile, you eat, drink, get well, eh?" He stood up, took the emptied bowl in his large, fleshy hands and walked away. "There's more in the kitchen with chicken and bread on the table," he said, then turned at the doorway. "Your name now, it's An…An..

"Anpaytoo."

"How about I call you Anya. eh? Easier for me to remember."

It was warm here; the linens and bedding were always snug, not ice cold as they were in the cabin across the road where they had been so brutally evicted. She had to give up her deerskin clothes and moccasins, which she folded and tucked away in the large dresser from which she removed her dresses. They were to be hung in the closet, according to Mrs. Zielinski, the elderly woman Casmir brought over to school Anya. Some of her dresses were new that Casmir had bought for her during the first few weeks of her stay, but the rest were from his late, stout wife that Anya had to alter to fit herself. And far in the back of the closet, she had made a stand where she hung the sacred bundle of Tasunke Paytah.

Anya would slip out of bed in the morning, quickly dress in a warm woolen skirt and long sleeved cotton blouse, stockings and leather shoes, pin her raven black hair back in a bun, and enter the kitchen where she cooked the breakfast of coffee, oatmeal or whatever old man Casmir ordered the night before. The kitchen was large with an ample wood stove. It didn't take long to get hot meals steaming on all four burners. She would wipe down the round table and place the plates and pewter ware on mats upon which cups of coffee gave off their aroma.

Casmir would stomp down from the upstairs room, "I see you're up early today, dziewcyna," he'd say while adjusting his shirt and belt around his portly frame as he entered the room. "That's good! That's good! You are a good little worker." He would pat her on the head and sit down, reaching with both hands for the utensils and shoveling the food into his mouth with a lusty fury.

While he was eating she would prepare his lunch of bread, cheese and a boiled egg, wrapping them in cloths and placing the bundle in a satchel that he carried. When he arose from the chair, he would wipe his chin with a napkin, then trudge over to the sink and wash his hands, wiping them on a towel that she had laid out for him. Then he would find his overcoat, which hung on one of the hooks in the hallway, lurch into them and his boots, don his cap, and smile at Anya, motioning goodbye, while he walked out, letting the door slam behind him.

After Casmir left, she would run into the living room and kneel on the overstuffed sofa, looking over its back and out the frosty, front window at what had once been her home across the street. *"Who needed the place so badly," she thought, "that we had to be roughly evicted in the middle of the winter?"* She watched for the newcomers in vain. The snowdrifts, piled high on the bushes, almost obscured the entryway. The wind whipped swirls of snow around like flimsy tops. She would sigh, remembering Takota, Hantaywee, Tokala Kohana and now deceased Tasunke Paytah. The pain over their separation was like a deep wound that would never heal.

The little house and the long pathway to the front porch was barely discernible behind the bushes. How often had she walked that path with Takota, sharing their happiness and laughing with the wind's eerie chant? And the garden that she and Hantaywee had tended, who would start it in the spring when the seeds they had saved were ready to be sown? She remembered Tokala Kohana, returning, drenched from the river, holding a string of fish they fried on the hot cast iron skillet. Jon Griswald and Tasunke Paytah had been there, too, along with Takotah. They pulled the chains of the ferry; then Tasunke Paytah left. *We tried hard to keep him close, to make him live with us, but his spirit deserted us long ago,* she thought.

When she sat back on the sofa to rest her eyes from the snowy glare, she noticed the picture in a rococo frame on the end table beside her. Casmir's deceased wife, Anastasia, better known as Anna, captivated anyone who looked at her arresting stare. Her dark brown hair, pulled back in a bun, accentuated her stern face, the mouth, a small, firm line above the small chin, the eyes, piercing and unforgiving under the straight brows. Yet, they had a touch of sadness in the furrows between them and in the creases at their edges even though her face was lightened by the photographer's rosy tint. The high necked collar of her dress was gathered together at the throat by a bronze medallion surrounded by tiny pearls; the dress, a grey-blue muslin, disappeared over her plump shoulders into the end of the portrait.

Anya's days were spent as if she were a captive, trapped in the locked house where she did the menial chores, dusting and polishing the furniture, scrubbing the floors, cleaning the rugs in the dining and living rooms with a carpet sweeper, and cooking the meals. On Monday mornings, Zeke's wife, Jana, would stop by to pick up the laundry, but she was a scrawny, sour-faced woman who looked at Anya with disdain as she carried the laundry basket out the door in the cold, blustering wind, her black shawl and dark dress leaving a long shadow behind her. When she returned with the clothes the next day, she would not say a word to Anya and even shunned her touch as she lay the basket at the doorway and turned to walk away to her home, the yellow clapboard house a few doors down. Anya would then spend the day ironing and darning the clothes.

27

PROGRESS

"Anya! Anya!" Open up!" It was Casmir one day at the back door, breathing heavily and lugging a heavy box into the house. She helped him lift and carry it into the parlor where he tore open the box to reveal "the new invention," he said, "a shuttle sewing machine. And here," he said, indicating the woman who walked in next to him, "Is your teacher, Mrs. Zielinski."

After that as Casmir left for work, Mrs. Zielinski knocked on the opened door and walked past him to stand over Anya. Mrs. Zielinski was a flinty instructor, who would sit down and show her how to push the shuttle and feed the material under the needle and thread. Anya observed the tall, angular woman peer over her beaked nose at her task while sitting stiffly at the machine and rhythmically moving her feet back and forth under her navy blue muslin skirt. "You see how relaxed you must be." She looked up at Anya who watched with faint amusement.

What's the rush?' Anya thought. *Were they expected to make a dress a day?* She sat at the machine as Mrs. Zielinski stood behind her, directed and maneuvered the cloth while Anya sewed with the magic of the movement of her feet rather than with the habit-formed quickness of her fingers. She felt clumsy using the machine, but as much as Anpaytoo avoided using it when she was alone, she responded with alacrity under the company of grim, dour Mrs. Zielinski.

After the warm, close, easy going relationships with her clan, the silence of her solitude and the ostracism of the surrounding Polish community was almost unbearable. While she went about her tasks in the grey stillness of the day, she would hum the songs that she and Hantaywee used to sing together in the garden while she longed for spring when she could cultivate the living, growing things again. She sang, a song from Red Bird that Takota used to sing. He said it was what he remembered from the Sundance he once was a part of when the Dakota, Lakota and Nakota lived together within the great forests and plains of what was now Minnesota.

"Grandfather/ a voice I am going to send/

hear me./ all over the universe/

a voice I am going to send./

Hear me,/ Grandfather,/

I will live./

I have said."

When Casmir left for work, letting the back door slam after him on a morning of the month they called April, the fresh scent of melting snow rushed in. Anya ran to open the front door, letting in the morning sun. The street was like a stream, sparkling with thin, cracking ice letting the waters flow. For the first time in months, Anya felt free as she walked down the front steps and around the corner to the backyard where the stable stood next to the thawing garden. When she entered it, the stable smelled of the old red roan, Hazel's, sweat and piles of hay.

She lifted a spade from among the tools hung on the stable wall and proceeded to the garden where she pulled open the heavy gate and began loosening the soil. Wet and muddy, the earth gave way beneath the metal tool as she pushed and dug with it. The soil was glistening with worms, that she turned up. *'Busier than me,'* she thought, *recalling her mother's satisfaction over such simple life forms, saying that they kept the earth "alive."* Throughout the morning she worked, planning the layout of the seeds, and when she was done, having replaced the spade and returned to the house, she drew her plan for the garden on a sheet of paper she found in Casmir's desk drawer. Life, nurturing life, the plants were to be arranged in families – beans, squash and corn — that would support each other. Her arms ached, stimulated by her labor, but she was glad.

After a simple lunch, she dragged the rugs out and onto the line in back where she proceeded to beat them while chanting a Dakota song: "Somewhere, someone is my friend. Somewhere, someone is my friend./ From above, a spotted eagle nation, do not doubt his power, he is my friend. Everyone behold! He comes to see me./ Somewhere someone is my friend. Somewhere, someone is my friend./ From the earth, a black tailed deer nation, do not doubt his power, he is my friend. Everyone behold! He comes to see me./ Somewhere someone is my friend. Somewhere, someone is my friend/From below, a mole nation, do not doubt his power, he is my friend. Everyone behold! He comes to see me./ Somewhere, someone is my friend. Somewhere, someone is my friend."

When done, she decided to wrap her cloak around her and take a brisk walk around the neighborhood, not being able to resist crossing the street to the old cabin. The garden needed to be rousted, and the front door was sagging. The eviction sign that had been posted was torn and flapping in the wind. She ripped it off and threw in on the ground, entering the place, finding it to be musty with lack of use. The kitchen table and chairs were covered with dust; the old stuffed sofa in the main room was cold and smelled of mildew; and the bed in the front bedroom was like a long yawning lap of emptiness.

She lingered on the river bank and gazed down at the ferry boat where it was moored. Her only connection now would be with mother earth during the times spent tilling the soil of the two gardens, which was cut short when she had to hurry back to clean and finish the indoor tasks before Casmir arrived so that she could serve him dinner. When he did arrive, he remarked upon the outdoor fragrance of the place from the windows she had opened, but insisted on closing them up tight, warning her about drafts and diseases, like head colds and the flu.

28

A SILENT SCREAM

On the day they called Monday when Zeke's wife Jana was especially surly, banging on the door as she left with the laundry and saying with a sneer, "We see you walking around, like you own the place. Well, you don't." and with that she slammed the door and traipsed down the street to her yellow house while followed by a gentle drizzle of rain from the overcast sky. Surprised by Jana's outburst, Anya began to consider the women she had met while detained among them. They were good women, but stern and unforgiving and even bitter. Mrs. Zielinski held herself so stiff and aloof, she didn't seem to have a natural bone in her body, while Jana was a storm cloud of fury. And yet Anya would see them laughing among themselves, especially if they were noticing something they thought was funny about someone they considered to be an outsider. They were like captives, trying to escape, but not finding a way out and amusing themselves in the meantime with cruel games and scurrilous observations. To Anya, the air was filled with morning birdsongs, the smell of the good, green earth with its abundance of fruits and vegetables, the sudden presence of ever abundant rabbits and deer, and the murmur of fish filled streams and rivers, lapping the shores with fresh replenishment; all of which were there for the taking— how could they be so unhappy? Her own greatest happiness was looking forward to seeing her mother, father and brother Tokana Kohala again.

Anya worked inside that morning, but was out the door the moment the rain stopped and the clouds parted revealing a brilliant blue sky with wisps of clouds, like gold-tinged, shredded white feathers. A westward wind rustled the tree tops and then swooped down below, sharing its breath with all growing things, including her. *Newly sprouting plants needed to be thinned and some replanted,* she thought, as she considered more mulch for the swales. She walked across the street toward the river bank to tend Hantaywee's garden, which basked in the sun and gave out the rich smell of the loamy soil beneath her that she mulched with soft hay from the backyard shed. Then while she collected wild berries and lemon balm for tea from the adjacent lot, she noticed how late it was for she saw the shadows falling westward.

Back at Casmir's garden, she completed the lattice work she had started around the fence to keep the squirrels and rabbits out. It was a complicated task, pounding the crosswork together in a way that the rodents couldn't wiggle through. Finally, she thought she had it set right, and she planted a few seeds of Morning Glory for its vines to wind around it, completing her handiwork. On her return to enter the house, she noticed the back door ajar and the screen door shaking in the wind; she berated herself for her carelessness. Tired, but in a good way, she walked over to the back steps, as she smiled with the joy of her work. Upon entering, she locked the back door and was about to hurry down the hallway while consumed with thoughts about what to make for supper.

"Going somewhere?" Zeke's gruff voice volleyed like a gunshot straight through her heart. She stopped and gasped at the sight of his tall, wiry form, a shadow at the end of the hall, that followed her as she turned, panic stricken, fighting off the grip of fear while she stumbled toward the back door and with shaking hands, fumbled with the lock. But her mind reeled with the shock of his heavy gait that echoed like a drumbeat in her head as he was upon her in an instant. Defiant, she faced him, trying to focus on controlling her fear, but in the fierce struggle that followed, she scratched his face, kicked, slammed her feet on the hallway walls, and bit deep into his knobby hands, broke his tensile grip and slipped out from under him; She raced toward the front door, smelling his foul breath behind her. Her heart beat so hard, she could feel it pounding throughout her body as she shrieked, ducked, dodged, threw dishes, a vase, which shattered at his feet, and, with trembling hands, pushed chairs between them. Zeke laughed, seized her, stifled her furious screeches with his mouth on hers, his spittle dripping down her cheeks, the veins on his neck pulsing with the effort while he grabbed both her arms and pulled her down beneath him. All she could recall was that with an intense, strenuous struggle, she almost broke away from the harness of him, but he slung his left fist back and slugged her unconscious.

When she came to, she realized that he had torn off her blouse, skirt and under garment, rendering her half naked. As if she were in a dream where you can't move she felt his salivating mouth on her bleeding lips which silenced her as she broke through her stupor, trying to yell,

"No!" But her scream was muffled behind her muzzled mouth while she felt him grunt and groan.

"What's going on here?" Casmir's rough voice racheted through her throbbing head. She felt Zeke release her body, letting her crumple to the floor, and she saw someone lift up Zeke by the shoulders and throw him against the wall, which shook with the impact while Zeke yelled, "She's nothin' but a redskin squaw!" the word catching in his throat like a squawk,

"Get out! Get out!" Casmir screamed and shoved him staggering out the front door. "Before I kill you"

He slammed the door shut and turned to Anya, who managed to drag herself up onto the sofa, nursing the left side of her face and gathering what remained of her skirt around her. "Oh my Anya!" He knelt next to her and tried to take her in his arms, but she pulled away.

"I want to leave this place," she muttered through swollen, split lips. "You must take me back to Hantaywee and Takota. I would rather starve with them than live one more day here." She stood up, gathered her torn skirt around her, and walked, wracked and rigid with pain, into the bedroom, closing the door behind her, where she tore off her bloodied clothes, crawled onto the bed and lay in a fetal position, naked under the covers. As if in an echo chmber, she heard Casmir rattle around in the kitchen, and she smelled the coffee he brewed while he made himself supper. Later she heard him stomp around the upstairs bedroom before he slept.

That night of the half moon, she wrapped herself in one of her old blankets, slipped out the door and stumbled across the street into the vacant lot where she followed the meadow with a gente slope down onto the riverbank; then she dropped her blanket and dove deep into the Mississippi's cool, pristine waters, swimming with its gentle current cleansing her face, caressing her bruised cheek, and rushing over her body; she surfaced, lay back on the bosom of the waves and let the living breathing waters carry her downstream. *'Oh death please take me,'* she thought, *wishing the waters would wash the ugliness out of her body and the intrusion out of her mind. 'Cover me and restore me through this river, this life blood of mother earth,'* she prayed, and would have let it carry her out to sea, and yet she turned and dove down deep to the bottom where life was primal and innocent. She wanted to join the weedy growth there where tiny beings moved hidden and untouched, but she could hold her breath no longer. With a shove upward, she broke through the water and gasped for air in the moonlight of that starry night.

The thought of returning to Takota and Hantaywee roused her enough for her to swim back upstream against the current. At the same time she considered Hantaywee's promise to her of the Ishna *Ta Awi Cha Lowan* (Her Alone They Sing Over), the ceremony that honored her because she was as sacred as the moon's tides to which she was joined. In the half moonlight, she resolutely pushed forward with the steady movement of her arms and legs, but at the same time her tears flowed with the images of the wooden cup, the cherries, sweet grass and sage, the holy pipe and tobacco dashed against the waves. When she swam ashore, emerged and covered herself with the blanket; she became aware that she was shaking, and her teeth were chattering.

As she returned to Casmir's she glanced at every shadow behind every tree, terrified, for she realized that her tormenter could be anywhere.

29

PLANS INTERRUPTED

Casmir pulled the old red roan to a stop at the edge of the town where he had last left Hantaywee and Takota. He had known then that they were doomed, which was why he dreaded the return. Anya, fully dressed in traditional buckskin and fur line moccasins, leaped down from the cart and ran toward the hillside, calling their names with her high, mellow voice reverberating against the crisp, brisk air. Casmir was about to turn the horse and cart around when loud, drawn out agonizing howls coming from the gravesite chilled him to the bone. He jumped down and headed in the direction of the ululating wails.

He found Anya, weeping at two gravesites, digging her hands into the earth and covering her face and hair with dirt. Her cries turned into a chant while she beat upon the ground and tore at her hair. Casmir stood speechless for a long time, until she noticed him, stopped, arose and confronted him.

"They've gone," she said with a break in her voice, her faced streaked with tears. "Tasunke Paytah's place is here," she said, indicating the scaffold where he lay. "Here lies Hantaywee." She sobbed and pointed toward her mother's shawl and beads on the next scaffold. "And there, Takota." She indicated his feathered hat and holstered knife, now rusted and she whispered, "Wicasa must have made these scaffolds for them." With a look of pure agony on her face, she gazed up at the sky while she pounded her fists on a hollow tree trunk, stamped on the ground and swayed in time with a mournful chant.

"Anya," Casmir stepped forward and clasped her hands in his. "You must come with me. I have thought of a plan, a way to protect you. Please, come with me. I will explain."

"I must find Wicasa," she whispered between clenched teeth while she wrenched her hands away from his grip. "I must know how this happened." She turned and ran toward Wicasa's cabin with Casmir stumbling along behind her, but when they reached the shack they found that it was empty. She turned and confronted him, her face, bruised and contorted with rage and grief and covered with grime streaked tears. "Your son killed them; your son and those men who threw us out of our house for no reason."

"I had nothing to do with that. I tried to help you. I even saved your life!" Casmir retorted. He looked down sheepishly, knowing how complicit the white community was.

But Anpaytoo ignored him while she searched the shelter. Wretched yet looking for signs of life, she touched Wicasa's ornaments and utensils.

"Nobody moved into our cabin." She muttered." The place is still empty and deserted. If we could have stayed the winter, we would have left for Canada by now." She turned, grabbed Casmir's shirt and stared wild eyed into his frightened ones. "Did you hear me, old man?" she screeched. "My parents starved to death because of your son and his friends." She let him go and turned away, disconsolate.

"Yes, yes, I heard you." Casmir gazed shamefaced at the ground. When he looked up he beseeched her with hands clasped. "Come with me, Anya. I have a plan for you that will save you from all this."

Anya backed away. "I will never leave here, never! Now go, old man! Go!" she screamed into his face while she shoved him. "Get away from me! I never want to see you again. Do you understand? Never!" Her face was laced with anguish.

30

PLANS UNFOLD

Casmir left only to return a week later with tall, bespectacled Dr. Ed Kasminski. "I could not leave her here among the dead," Casmir said. Anya could hear their muffled conversation outside the hut.

They trudged several yards away to where they entered Wicasa's ramshackle shack under another stand of trees where Anya was aware that both of them were leaning over her as she lay on Wicasa's straw cot. The doctor's hands were cold on her temples and her wrist as he bent over her.

"Her hair is chopped off and disheveled, her lips are cracked, but she's still alive. How did she get that bruise on the left side of her face? What's worse is that she could die from starvation and exposure out here. She's already alarmingly thin," he said. The cot moved with the doctor's weight on it where he sat down and Anya felt his strong hands under her head.

"Here, take this," he ordered. His voice was firm and reassuring. She swallowed, grimacing at the taste of the bitter liquid. She watched him, from under her half closed eyelids as he stood, a blurry figure, and gave Casmir a flask.

"Have her take this laudanum whenever she gets restless. Have her take it until she heals" He bent down over her and turned her limp body. "Look here where she had wounds, blood caked cuts on her arms. These must be washed and swathed"

"Was she trying to kill herself?" Casmir leaned over; and she saw what looked like his distorted face as she fell into a deep sleep.

While she lay, covered with blankets and jouncing with the wagon, Casmir and the doctor discussed her case in barely discernible undertones. Helpless, she watched as the two birches, markers of the village that once was, faded away in the distance

"Come come, now." Mrs. Zielinski's petulant muttering penetrated Anya's slumbering form under the covers *where she dreamt of brilliant green and golden meadows melting into a dense black forest where she wandered, crying out for Takota and Hantaywee. The saplings bent down to brush their soft leaves against her as she wandered under an azure sky, blending into a overarching, radiant rainbow. Wicasa appeared dancing on the red road emerging from the forest, the fringes of his buckskin breeches swaying in the wind. He had painted yellow lightening on his chest and his face, half red, half black. His necklace of wolves' teeth jangled against his chest while he swayed in the forest, pounding on his drum softly to soothe her.*

"It is a time for the long battle, Anpaytoo," he chanted while singing the war dance song. "You must join us. We are fighting for our lives throughout this land. Many of us will die, but for those who live, you must fight for us; never give up the struggle."

As Anya felt the movement of the earth beneath her, she awoke instead to the smell of clean sheets, quilts and comforters being rearranged around her. Her head rested on a plump pillow where Mrs. Zielinski was slipping her bony hand under her shoulders, lifting her to receive a spoonful of medicine. Anya gagged and choked on the liquid. "Come, come, now", Mrs. Zielinski insisted, administering the liquid until Anya fell back in a swoon, but not quite asleep, she overheard Casmir as he entered the room.

"The cuts and bruises are gone from her face now, and her arms are healing," he said as she felt his hands on her arms and face. "And her hair is growing back." She felt his hands smoothing down the ragged strands. "She must eat. She needs more than bread dipped in soups and liquids."

Mrs. Zielinski nodded and gathered up the utensils, leaving a napkin underneath Anya's chin in case she needed more medicine. The tall, plain, elderly widow was a steadfast servant, quick and wary, who would have accepted a proposal from Casmir without hesitation, were it not for this recalcitrant girl who had bewitched him, *who was too young for him*, she thought, while carrying the tray of utensils to the kitchen. If she served him long enough, he would see that. He would see that a woman closer to his age would give him more stability, more practical wisdom, which would guide him in his work. For now, though, she accepted the paltry wages he gave her, taking them back with her to subsist at the home her late husband had left her.

When Anya was healed enough to sit on the sofa, Mrs. Zielinski would bring her a tray of food, sigh impatiently, and then bustle about with the housework. Anya began to eat and continue the struggle, as Wicasa had said she must in her dreams. To her astonishment, she had become ravenously hungry, but at the same time, nauseated enough to vomit into a pail she found in the kitchen. The life that coursed through her body overcame these episodes, and she was finding it difficult to fit into her own clothes. The oversized dresses of Casmir's late wife, Anna, were beginning to fit her better. *What was she becoming, she wondered.*

"You must understand. Zeke was not raised in the normal way." Casmir was saying as they both sat together on the sofa one day with Anya lost in a laudanum fog. His voice seemed far off, as in a dream. "The Atlantic Ocean crossing over here on the ship was hard on my wife; she took ill and died while giving birth to Zeke when we arrived here. So I had to hire that old crone, Mrs. Zelda Wisniewski, down the street to take care of him while I worked. Crazy Mrs. Wisniewski kept telling the boy that he killed his mother. One day he comes to me. 'Papa,' he says, 'did I kill mama?' No, I say and I tell that old woman to stop telling him that. I don't know if she did or not. He's not right in his head, my boy. I am sorry."

Anya remembered these things as she drowsily drifted into the blissful sleep of laudanum. The dreams, resplendent with color and Wicasa's mesmerizing chants, reoccurred often enough to make her hunger for them. When she awoke, now and then, she discovered that it was daybreak and she realized that she was at Casmir's house. Often he was sitting beside her, usually on Sundays when he stayed with her, keeping a close watch.

During the days that followed, he accepted her erratic routine. Sometimes breakfast or supper would be served, sometimes not. At times there would be evidence of her having tended the garden, at times there would not. The doors were always locked when he returned from work as were the windows. No more fresh breezes greeted him, although, at times, springs of parsley, cilantro, chopped carrots, onions, and celery would be laid out on the table, ingredients for a savory soup. As her bruises healed, her appetite seemed to have returned and increased to the point where Casmir noticed the thickening of her waist and how ponderous her steps were becoming.

"Anya," he said one evening, calling her into the living room, where he indicated that she be seated on the sofa. She looked down at the handmade dress she had sewn out of the gingham he had bought her. In slow motion, she sat as if she were trying to get used to her developing body. Next to her, on the end table was the picture of Casmir's late wife with her heavy brows and figure. "I remember my wife, Anna, how she looked before she had Zeke, and you are in the same condition." He stopped to clear his throat. "But I know of a way I can protect you. You see," he continued, pressing his hands against his shirt and trousers to smooth them. "I love you." His voice quavered. "I've loved you since the first moment I set eyes on you. Why else do you think I saved you from your mother and father's fate? I did not want any harm to come to you, and I have an ache in my heart over how you have already been harmed."

While she looked at his round face, she thought *that everything about him was round.* His eyes were deep set under round brows over his bulbous nose, pursed mouth and rotund body. Though he carefully trimmed his grey beard and pointed goatee, even that did not offset his softness.

She watched him feel in his vest pocket and pull out a box. Fumbling, he dropped it in his lap, but picked it up and opened it to reveal a thin, silver ring. "Will you marry me?" He slipped the ring on her finger. She lifted her hand to the light and gazed at the ring's small silver stone, gleaming in the sunlight. She looked at him inquisitively.

"If you marry me, Anya, you will be protected. You will have my name, and these Polish people, the priest, everyone, will join together to guard you." He held up his hands as if calling them all to surround them. "No one will touch Mrs. Wojcik."

She let her hand down onto her lap and looked into his grey eyes. "but what will they say about a man who marries an Indian?"

"That's the beauty of it. I have them convinced that you're a Polish woman of Tatar descent from the Steppes whose husband died on the trip over here."

"Tatar?"

"Dark and exotic looking, not fair like most of us, they came from the East and invaded Poland and intermarried. They may even be your ancestors, since some of them went the other way into Asia" He leaned forward. "And besides, you must know by now that you will have a child. Married to me, that child and you will be treated with respect. Otherwise, you will be cast off, a whore. I don't know if I could protect you then." He lifted her chin so that he could look into her coal black eyes. "So please marry me, Anya."

She looked away, then gazed at the ring, sparkling in the sunlight, while thoughts swarmed in her head about what a web of lies he was weaving. *How could she allow herself to be caught up in them? But then she realized that she already was embedded in the silver trap of the ring, for how would she survive if she were cast away alone into the wilderness? How could she have a child there with no elder women to guide her? with no tribal community to protect her? Even the wolves had each other. There was no way out but to survive, to live, as her mother had insisted.* She lowered her head, hesitated for a moment, then looked up, "Yes," she said, "I will marry you."

"Good," he said, standing up. "I will contact my brother Andrew and his wife Constance in Winona.

31

A CHANGELING

In a laudanum fog, Anya sat next to Casmir in the wagon while he drove his red roan, Hattie, down the winding road to Winona, Minnesota, where a Polish settlement flourished around its Basilica of St. Stanislaus built with the help of a small mission of Franciscan priests. He had taken her to Winona a few months ago to stay with his brother Andrew and his wife, Constance, who had settled down there. They agreed to oversee her care so that she could be instructed in the faith. It had been early spring then, and the blossoms were budding on the lilacs while wild roses were coming into full bloom. The farmland stretched for miles in which the settlers had set to work, tilling and working the soil, leaving squares of home vegetable gardens and acres of cash crops of grain side by side. Horses and cows grazed in the open fields next to the rustic barns and tidy, clapboard homes.

At the time, Anya knew that by going south, they were jogging farther away from Takota's originally intended home in Canada. She felt a pull toward the north, but they were heading south into the terrain she once knew intimately. It was a dissonance she could barely manage, for in her mind, the natural surroundings in Minnesota that she had once lived in had disappeared into a loveless, barren wastelend. The woodland she had cherished were fast disappearing along with the joy of discovering the natural plants and berries that grew under its canopy. The world that she once knew had been a captivating home where she dwelt with her nation and their holy man, Wicasa, who taught her to honor the great mother earth, for it was sacred. Clearing the forest from the land and discarding what was not profitable in favor of cultivating crops for sale was strange to her for she had felt related to every living, growing thing. Their removal felt like a personal loss of friends and providers, guardians of the soil and the creatures who dwelt there, including her tribe.

We were part of the community of the natural world, she thought and remembered *Wicasa with his eagle feathers, buckskin leggings and bear claw necklace, wearing a buffalo-horned headdress and robe, telling her his stories filled with a wisdom she longed for now that he was gone. "You must give, even if it hurts, even if it seems like the most precious thing in the world to you," he said about her little pony during her naming ceremony. And so her cherished golden pony was given to a little boy in the camp who needed it. His delight was something she never forgot.*

"So you, Anpaytoo Hanwi (Radiant Moonlight), have become the seed that opens and grows into a great tree," said Wicasa, marveling over how straight and tall she stood as she handed over the reins without complaint. He echoed

the sayings made by many wise women and men before him that through her suffering, she was becoming someone of great influence.

She nodded in a half-sleep, recalling the priest who had instructed her in the Catholic religion, tall, lean Father Pietrowski, who that first day had sat across from her at his shabby, yet somewhat officious looking desk, took her hands in his and locked his bright blue eyes onto her somber ones. "You are not a Tatar," he said. "You are an Indian, a Sioux, I would guess."

"Dakota," she corrected.

He spoke a few words to her in Dakota, evoking a surprised look in her eyes. "My fondest wish was to be a missionary among your people," he said in his brusque voice. "So I was assigned here years ago, and just as I was beginning to reach your people, they reassigned me to this parish." She looked at his earnest face and wondered why he was confiding to her in this way. *He must be hoping that he can 'reach' me,* she thought.

Now as autumn's glory surrounded them, giving death from life its due, Casmir was driving her to Winona on their wedding day, followed by a small caravan that made up part of the wedding party. The fields were barren and yet showed signs of the abundant harvest in the stacks of grain lying like mounds of gold across the land, What was left of the summer's heat cooled by the west winds, enabled Anya to recall Casmir's account of his meeting with the pastor after she had "graduated" from his class and was a full-fledged, baptized and confirmed Catholic.

"She is a remarkable young woman, your bride to be," the priest had told Casmir while seated across from him behind his desk and forming his long hands into a triangle. "You say she comes from the Steppes of Poland? That she is Tatar?'

Casmir had shrugged. (*How could he lie to a priest?* he thought)

"Well…" The lanky priest in his black cassock leaned back in his chair, and with his hands clasped behind his head, stared up at the ceiling for awhile. "She doesn't seem to be of the Muslim faith. She seems to be more or less influenced by the Indians, the Dakotas, to be exact. But, then, she speaks Polish fluently. Remarkable that she can speak three languages fluently."

"Oh she came here very young," Casmir had tried to explain. "So, yes, she could have some of the Indian beliefs. I don't know. She has worked for me for only a few years."

The priest had lowered his arms and leaned forward. "It's amazing how she has kept her presence of mind, orphaned and widowed at such a young age," he continued. "I appreciate the kindness of your brother Andrew and his wife, Constance, taking her in as they did here in Winona. As far as her religious instruction goes, which, as you know, I have given personally as a favor to you. (*Casmir nodded while thinking that the favor was in return for his money.*) I would say that she's quick to learn. For one thing, she has no problem with the notion of eternal life. 'Our ancestors are all around us,' she said, when I told her about the communion of saints. And she readily accepted the seven sacraments, since her people have seven sacred ceremonies, too. They are different and yet similar in that they mark the passages of life, as do ours."

"When we read the scriptures, she took to the story of Jesus, our Savior, rapidly, uttering some Dakota words I barely understood. He's apparently a sacred holy man to her, and she was visibly shaken by his death. She had difficulty with the doctrines of the Trinity and Original Sin, though. To her there was only one Great Spirit, Wakan Tanka, who oversees and sustains everything. And yet, she believes in one Creator God, she speaks of the Holy Spirit over us all, and she loves Jesus. So she can't be far from the truth."

"As for sin, she knows of evil and has a highly structured moral sense, from absolute honesty and sharing of goods to respect for the ownership of others and honoring one's elders." The priest then pushed a diagram of a triangle across the desk. "As you know this shows the levels of creation, with God above it. At the top of the pyramid are the angels," he said, indicating their place on the visual, "then man, who is just a little below the angels, then the animal kingdom, then the plants, and lowest of all, the inanimate rocks and minerals of the earth." He watched while Casmir bent over the large diagram and looked up.

"She didn't accept this. That there are gradations and that man was meant to subdue the earth were beyond her. To her, creation was in the form of a circle, which she drew here." The priest pushed across Anya's crude drawing for Casmir to see. "She said that we were all on the same level except the Great Spirit, who was everywhere and who made everything sacred. I thought that could not be reconciled with Catholic teaching until, as a Franciscan, myself, I remembered St. Francis of Assisi who related to nature as family, a holy one at that." The priest stood up, his ascetic face drawn as if about to deliver a verdict. "And so I determined that she is eligible for baptism and the sacraments. After all, at this point she knows more than the children we instruct, and like them, we expect her to grow in the faith, so why not."

Casmir had lifted up his hands with relief.

"I recommend that she be baptized as soon and possible with Confirmation and First Communion soon to follow," said the priest, standing and walking around the desk to Casmir, who was arising to meet him. They shook hands.

"Oh yes, Father Pietrowski, It will be arranged." Casmir could hardly contain his joy.

While ushering him out the door, the priest murmured, "And I would have the marriage performed shortly afterwards." He lowered his voice and looked directly into Casmir's eyes, "considering her condition." Of course, Casmir thought, how could he not have noticed her rapid weight gain these last few months?

32

THE WEDDING

When Anya stood in the late Anastasia's wedding gown before the sanctuary of the ornate, white marble and gold canopy of the altar of the Polish church of St. Stanislaus in Winona; she looked down at the flowing, white mass of satin around her and felt like a ruffled swan about to take off. Casmir, who was aware of her unease, stood beside her, guiding her through the ceremony. His brother, Andrew, the best man, stood beside him while Jana, the maid of honor, stood at Anya's right side. The church smelled of flowers and candle wax. The iconic statues in their niches and the figures depicted in the stained glass windows seemed to revel in a dazzling array of colors.

Father Pietrowski followed the ritual without a misstep. He stood in his priestly attire with his shock of tawny hair brushed back and smiled indulgently while he watched the wedding party: Casmir's daughter-in-law and her three children, strode with pomp down the aisle. Jana's boy, the ring bearer, led the procession. In his suit he walked like a little man, entrusted with the wedding rings on a small pillow. His two little sisters, dressed in white, like miniature brides, had strolled behind him, strewing flower petals on the aisle. Their mother, Jana, followed and watched her charges with fierce concentration. Anya entered on the arm of thin, dignified, bespectacled Dr. Kasminski with his mustache trimmed and his iron grey hair brushed back,. A crowd of neighbors were there as was the infamous Mrs. Wisniewski, whose plump and wizened face peered past that of the faithful servant, Mrs. Zielinski. Zeke, mercifully, did not attend. The organ had blared accompanied by the choir's voices reverberating throughout the echoing acoustics of the church.

Anya did not remember much of the ceremony nor of the Latin mass that was interwoven, except a portion of the readings which were in Polish. She recalled that the priest read from the Epistle to the Ephesians: "Brethren: Let women be subject to their husbands as to the Lord; for the husband is the head of the wife, as Christ is the head of the Church…. let every one of you in particular love his wife as himself, and let the wife fear her husband." In another reading, the Gospel of Matthew: "For this cause shall a man leave his father and mother, and shall cleave to his wife,. What, therefore, God hath joined together, let no man put asunder." *She thought it strange that she should fear Casmir and be subject to him and stranger still, that they should leave their parents.*

Anya was comforted by her small part in the ceremony. All she and Casmir had to do was to say, "I will" to the question the good priest asked each of them. "Casmir wilt thou take Anya here present, for thy lawful wife, according to the rite of our holy Mother the Church?" And then "Anya wilt thou take…." After obtaining this consent, he asked them to join their right hands and to repeat after him their pledge to each other to "take thee for my lawful spouse to have and to hold from this day forward, for better or for worse, for richer, for poorer, in sickness and in health, until death do us part…."

Father Pietrowski then prayed in Latin, "Ego conjugo vos in matrimonium, in nomine Patris, + et Filii, et Spiritus Sancti. Amen." (I join you together in marriage, in the Name of the Father, + and of the Son, and of the Holy Ghost. Amen}" He then blessed them and their rings, sprinking them with holy water, and guided the couple while they put the rings on each other's third finger of the left hand, saying to each other, "With this ring, I thee wed…" The mass continued with the community participating in the Eucharist until at last, Father Pietrowski motioned for the couple to turn, and he announced, "I now pronounce you, Casmir and Anya, man and wife!" At that Casmir grabbed Anya and kissed her hard upon the mouth. The organist struck up the wedding march while Anya and Casmir and the wedding party triumphantly strode down a few steps and away from the altar. But when the couple was halfway down the aisle, the music and choir paused and then broke into the lively mazurka of the Polish National Anthem:

Jeszcze Polska nie umarła,

Kiedy my żyjemy

Co nam obca moc wydarła,

Szablą odbijemy.

Poland has not yet died/

So long as we still live/

What the alien power had seized from us/

We shall capture with a sabre../

Chorus:

Marsz, marsz, Dąbrowski

Do Polski z ziemi włoskiej

Za twoim przewodem

Złączym się z narodem

March, march Dobrowski,/

To Poland from the Italian land./

Under your command /

We shall rejoin the nation./

Jak Czarniecki do Poznania

Wracał się przez morze

Dla ojczyzny ratowania

Po szwedzkim rozbiorze

Like Czarniecki to Poznan/

Returned across the sea/

To save his homeland/

After the Swedish partition./

Marsz, marsz...

March, march...(chorus)/

Przejdziem Wisłę, przejdziem Wartę

Będziem Polakami

Dał nam przykład Bonaparte

Jak zwyciężać mamy

We'll cross the Vistula and the Warta,/

We shall be Polish./

Bonaparte has given us the example/

Of how we should prevail./

Marz, marz...

March, march (chorus)/

Niemiec, Moskal nie osiędzie,

Gdy jąwszy pałasza,

Hasłem wszystkich zgoda będzie

I ojczyzna nasza

The German nor the Muscovite will settle/

When with backsword in hand,/

"Concord" will be everybody's watchword/

And so will be our fatherland./

Marz, marz...

March, march... (chorus)/

Już tam ojciec do swej Basi

Mówi zapłakany

Słuchaj jeno, pono nasi

Biją w tarabany

A father, in tears,/

Says to his Basia/

Listen, our boys are said/

To be beating the tarabans./

Marz, marz...

March, march...(chorus)/

Na to wszystkich jedne głosy

Dosyć tej niewoli

Mamy racławickie kosy

Kościuszkę Bóg pozwoli.

All exclaim in unison,/

"Enough of this slavery"/

We've got the scythes of Raciawice,/

God give us Kosciuszko."

The crowd greeted them on the steps outside throwing rice and calling out, "Stolat!" while they rushed with a whirl of convergence into their carriages and wagons to escort the couple to the dance hall where the festivities began. While seated in the carriage Casmir had rented for the occasion, Anya turned to him and asked, "What did they mean in the song, "Jeszcze Polska nie umarła,/Poland has not yet died/ Kiedy my żyjemy,/ So long as we still live?"

"Didn't you know?" He looked at her exotic face. "But then, of course, how could you. The land of Poland is no more, but the nation still lives."

"How can that be?"

"We were the greatest nation in Europe, until King Boleslaw divided the kingdom among his sons, and then we were at war for centuries until we joined with Lithuania. But even then with the support of that nation, Poland was diminished." He paused while Anya looked on intently. "Our problem was with the Sjem," She looked puzzled. "The sjem was like a council or congress here, but there, it gave the nobles too much power and allowed them to elect the king – first one was from France, then other nations. It was downhill from there." Casmir looked off in the distance. "The surrounding nations, Russia, Germany, Austria, invaded Poland and divided it up according to their claims. The nation of Poland is no more – for hundreds of years, but the land is not the nation. The people are. We still have our language, God, our love of freedom, We the people, will never let go of our heritage; Poland still lives in us." He pressed his fist against his chest.

"The Dakota no longer have their land, either," said Anya.

"But that is different. They never had it to begin with. They just lived on it. They are not a nation." Casmir said, while Anya stared at him with disbelief.

Before she could respond, the carriage had stopped in front of a large clapboard building. Upstairs was the dance hall they entered after passing through the anteroom, which was festooned with tables covered with gifts and a buffet of food. A band on a stage at the far end of the ballroom was already playing polkas and mazurkas with a few waltzes in between. The accordion gave it a distinctive flair as the couples stamped the schottische and whirled around on the wooden dance floor. To Anya fell the task of carrying her wedding dress skirt folded around her right arm so that it formed a large catchall where the men could throw their envelopes with their offerings after they'd danced with her. Some threw in bills and coins. Women also threw in their monetary gifts, all of which she emptied into a large basket that Casmir brought to her.

Children wandered in and out among the dancers; some of them danced with Anya, lifting their tow heads to see the beautiful face of the glowing bride with the raven black hair and eyes, she who looked at them with a bit of a crooked smile. After a brief respite when Anya had a bite to eat, Casmir signaled that this was his dance, the last one with her.

"What do you mean, the Dakota are not a nation?" she asked, her cheeks flushed with anger. "We're a great nation!" She reiterated while they whirled around in a waltz.

"Are you still thinking about that?" Casmir laughed. "OK. They were a nation, but not anymore. And that is all I will say. Now I know why my papa told me not to talk politics with a woman." He laughed all the more at her smoldering eyes.

While they were leaving, stepping down the stairs outside the entryway, two men shouted out in Polish, "Hey Casmir, where's Zeke?

"Since when did he stop being your son?"

"He had to work, today," Casmir shouted back.

"Oh yeah? How come before I left, I saw him at Nowak's bar, eh?"

"That Raspunik! He probably wanted your new bride for his own playtoy," joined in one of the women with them.

Casmir told Anya to ignore them while they entered the coach that took them to his brother's place. At Andrew and his wife Constance's house, a dinner had been prepared for the couple, and a bevy of women and families gathered around them with gifts. A young girl stood in the parlor with an accordion, playing Polish music while they sang along. They entered upon the soft red and gold oriental carpet that spread throughout the living and dining rooms and beneath the heavy, dark oaken furniture where it seemed to muffle the conversations of the small crowd. The children were racing around outdoors, making their joyful noises. Anya felt as uncomfortable sitting on the plush sofa as she did with her new baptismal name, Anya, which Casmir said was a formality. If they only knew the meaning of my true name, she thought, how careful my parents and elders were when choosing it, seeing in her a brilliant light in the vast, dense wilderness that surrounded them, defining her for who she really was.

They gathered around the kitchen table where the feast was laid out: chicken, rosol (chicken noodle soup) kopytka (potato chunks), golabki (stuffed cabbage rolls),beef and mizeria (cucumber salad). In the middle was a large fruit cake which the buxom Mrs. Wisniewski sliced and served with coffee or tea after they'd eaten. The couple sat at the head of the dining room table table, surrounded by Casmir's grandchildren and former in-laws. Some of the guests spilled out into the living room and ate their meal while they sat on the sofa or nearby stuffed chairs.

As the guests left, Mrs. Wisniewski and Jana cleared the table and cleaned the dishes with a clatter that accompanied Casmir's long goodbyes to those who lingered on the front steps. Anya smiled at them, but remained demurely quiet while longing to release her feet from the tight new leather, button up shoes that Jana had bought her. When the last guest had left, Mrs. Wisniewski and Jana Wojcik untied their aprons and gathered their shawls around them. While making ready to leave, Jana tarried behind the older woman and stopped on the steps to say with wrinkled, pursed lips, "So you are a Tatar convert, eh? How does it feel to be a Christian?" She examined Anya's face for the tell tale signs of uncertainty that she expected with a fabrication.

Anya looked into Jana's pale blue eyes under a head crowned by hair the color of the sun

"I don't remember being a Tatar," she said.

Satisfied, since Anya did not flinch, Jana said. "But you must know something. Tell me is it true that Muslims eat Christians?" She laughed at Anya's startled look, but stout-bodied Mrs. Wisniewski intervened, grabbed Jana by the arm and pulled her away while she chided her for saying such a thing on Anya's wedding day.

"A thousand apologies," Mrs. Wisniewski said, scowling with displeasure. Walking Jana and her brood down the steps and front pathway, she continued to scold Jana as they strode away under the stars to their farm wagons that they would ride back to Minneapolis in the darkness of a quarter moon.

After their goodbyes, Anya's and Casmir's wagon soon followed. They travelled in the dead of night with a soft, early autumnal breeze blowing and haystacks from the harvest dotting the fields like prehistoric mounds in the moonlight. Instead of happiness, Anya felt a deep sadness and confusion. She had not understood what the ceremony meant and noticed with dread the macabre smile on Mrs. Zielinski's thin face while she watched Casmir take Anya's arm before they walked from the altar where Fr. Pietrowski had wed them. Though the wedding party made merry, their greetings felt hollow and insincere. And now she was sitting next to a lewd old man who posed as her savior.

They drove on in the dark until Casmir's home on the horizon was a welcome sight to Anya. After he guided the old red roan into the barn where Casmir unhitched the sweating horse and bedded her stall with fresh hay; they walked down the pathway to Casmir's ramshackled house, entered and closed the door with a click. "Do you see how they accept you now?" he said as he turned to her, his cheeks shining under the lantern he held. "You can walk among them and not be afraid." She yawned unexpectedly. "But you must be tired," he said. "We will talk in the morning." He led her to her room, his large, fleshy palm under her elbow, and opened the door for her. "Do you see, Anya, how they have changed?" He tried to make eye contact, but she stared past him as if in a dream. He shrugged and said, "You get plenty of rest now, so that you can give birth to our child." With the lantern wick, he lit the candles on the end tables and left to make his way upstairs.

In the semi darkness redolent with the faint smell of candle smoke, Anya sat on the edge of the bed, unbuttoned and slipped off her shoes and sighed with relief as she shoved them under the bed. She glanced at the two hurricane glass covered candles on the end tables on each side of the bed, unaware that Jana and Mrs. Wiesniewski had left them there, expecting the couple to share the bed that night. She made her way to the dresser, took out the moccasins she had stored there, and slipped them onto her feet. The cumbersome dress and her undergarments were next and they were soon lying in a heap, which she gathered up and stuffed into the closet. No sooner had she put on her white cotton nightgown when she heard something moving in the living room.

With candle in hand she entered the room and felt the presence of spirits, just as she had felt the ghost-spirit with her mother in the old cabin. There were echoes of an accordion and the faint image of another musical instrument, which looked like an upright dresser with accordion keys lined along the front with someone sitting there and singing in a quivering soprano voice. Others were there, sitting on the sofa and chairs, eating, conversing and laughing.

She stood in the middle of the room whirling around while the candle made myriads of shadows on the walls until the music and specters disappeared.

Returning to her room, she pulled off her moccasins, let them fall on the floor, and snuggled under the covers on the bed where she lay awake for awhile, reflecting on the journey she had made and her participation in a ritual that was strange to her. She had not planned on signing up to be "subject" to Casmir. From her mother's teachings and the tribe's attitude towards its women, she had always thought that she had a special role to play in their scheme of things, and, to them, that role was sacred. She was meant to be a holy woman, a wisdom keeper and teacher to generations of her children and an example for them to follow in the tradition of the White Buffalo Woman who had given them their seven sacred rituals. To be "subject" to her spouse was an entirely new concept to her. But at this time, she could not bring herself to object to anything in the Christian ritual, for contending with the threat of Zeke, his proximity, and the loss of her parents was enough for her. How she wished she had found Wicasa for he would have rescued her and explained everything to her. After snuffing out the candles, she drifting off to sleep while mulling over Anastasia's clothing that she would have to adjust and make larger this time

33

WHAT CHILD IS THIS? (1876-1880)

"Push! Push! Puuuush!" The yell rebounded as if awakening her from a nightmare where she was lost, calling for help, unheeded, at the bottom of a far off canyon. Anya heard Helga, the midwife, while she, herself, cried out on the birthing bed in the small, yellow clapboard house on Pritchard Street. As the searing pain wrenched through her body, Anya tried to sit up, her disheveled hair falling about her shoulders; her face wet with perspiration. She wanted to run into the woods, to kneel, to squat, anything but lie flat on her back while the midwife pulled on the infant struggling for its life withn her. The struggle between the two woman became like a wrestling match; at one time both of them locked hands, and shoved against each other. Helga's lean and wiry assistant, Norma, stepped in to break them apart and help Helga restrain Anya. With a strength she did not know she had, Anya shoved them both away again and again as she strove to sit upright, to let Mother Earth's forces assist her, but instead, the midwife and Norma eased Anya down on her back, her limbs slippery with sweat, her body wracked and weak with the agony of the struggle.

Helga's round, ruddy face hovered above with her reddish blond hair combed back into a net. She was a stout woman, dressed in blue and white, her starched skirts rustled, crisp and fresh smelling when she bustled about the room. The sleeves of her blouse were pushed up her rotund arms while she bent over Anya, urging her not to give up, as she worked her hands into the birth canal to position the emerging infant. The assistant brought towels and clean sheets to slip under Anya, fussing over her, who thrust them away trying to birth her baby in peace.

With one tremendous burst of energy, she sat up, squatted on the bed and with a long, loud scream, reaching a crescendo that trailed off — the infant was released into her hands where she held it and stared at it, her hair falling about her arms in wet disarray.

"Mrs. Wojcik, you MUST lie down," Helga cried out while she gently pushed and repositioned Anya on her back. "I need to take the baby and cleanse it," the midwife continued, motioning to her assistant to bring the instrument that she used to cut the umbilical cord.

"I want that," Anya cried out, sitting up on her elbows

"This? Helga looked at Anya with astonishment. "Nobody cares about the afterbirth."

"I must bury it," whispered Anya, and then lay back, realizing where she was and why the midwife did not understand. But Helga wrapped it in a cloth and put it aside.

Norma approached Anya with the clean and newly swaddled infant. "You have given birth to a little boy," she said with a smile. But Anya had dropped off to sleep after her twenty-four hour long ordeal.

The days that followed seemed to be enveloped in a delicate mist. Led down the front steps of Helga's small house, Anya held the tiny, swaddled infant close to her heart while Casmir took her down the street in his wagon. Once inside his familiar home, she rested on the sofa and breast fed the boy she called Fierce Storm, but Casmir named him Stanley.

"It was my father's name," he said. "I let Anastasia name the other one after the prophet, Ezekiel, from her bible studies. She had high ideals for her boy. Too high "

He shrugged, as if the name made no difference. "My father was a good man. I think it'll help give God another chance," He took one look at the disapproval in her face and added firmly, "We'll call him Stan."

"Stan." She repeated while thinking, how dull the name was. The name, Fierce Storm, said much more about his entrance into the world. She bent her head down to look at the tiny waif in her arms; who struggled, wrinkled his face and let out a yowl whenever he needed something. Anya laughed, lifting him up, so that he too would smile, holding him close, so that he too would feel comforted. She cared for him in ways that were both constant and playful and began early on, carrying him around with her and showing him things, telling him their names. The boy was never out of her sight.

34

A STRANGE NEW LIFE

As Casmir had predicted, the community accepted Anya as his wife, and Jana was more civil toward her. As the months moved on, Anya had noticed a faint familiarity in Stan's features, and she recoiled when he began to show a remarkable resemblance to Zeke. Though she still felt delight with the baby, a cold reserve began to overshadow her feelings toward him, which she felt deeply but could not overcome.

Casmir would chuckle when neighborhood visitors would comment on the resemblance. "He's my second chance, son," he would say with a guffaw, expressing his confidence that this child would be "right in the head." But the neighbors continued to gossip about the child who looked more like his supposedly half brother, Zeke, than Casmir. Heads would nod as they whispered in groups that Stan looked more like Casmir's first wife, Anna, whom Zeke favored.

Jana came over once and awhile to see Casmir's "second chance baby," as she called him, and she would wonder, loudly, why Anya spent so much time with "the kid," and why she carried him around with her wherever she went.

"Put him on a schedule," Jana said. "Free yourself. Leave him in his crib and do your work. It would go faster and you wouldn't be distracted by him," she advised,

"Schedule?" said Anya, "Free myself? But why? We are both free together. And he is good company. He cries when he's alone. Wouldn't he be lonely in the crib all by himself? And how would he learn anything there?" Ingrained in Anya was the need to keep her baby secure and to help him get used to the world he was entering into.

Jana shook her head. "And when he gets older, you must make him obey you even if you have to spank him."

"Spank?" Anya did not understand.

"Surely you must know what a spanking is." Jana stared at her in disbelief. "It means that you hit him – right there on his little butt." Jana laughed with a voice that was as grating as steel wool on a pot. "You Tatars certainly know nothing about how to raise a kid," she exclaimed. "'Spare the rod and spoil the kid,' that's what we always say," she contended with a pursed mouth while looking down her beaked nose at Anya.

"Hit him? Why?" Anya held the boy close and shook her head. "He is a wakhanheza (a sacred being)." But Jana was insistent and repeated her instructions as she left. Anya closed the front door on what she knew would be the petty gossip of the neighborhood.

The following months were spent fending off Jana's nasal nagging that Anya conform to Jana's child rearing practices. At times Anya wished she could escape the confines of the neighborhood with its boxes of houses that were beginning to line the street. When Mrs. Wisniewski came barging out her door and Anya saw her headed in her direction, stopping to glare at her over the fence while she was in the garden, she would excuse herself with, "Oh no! I left a pot of soup cooking on the stove," and would carry little Stanley into the kitchen where she would rock him and distract him until Mrs. Wisniewski was nowhere in sight.

He was wrapped in the muslin sling around her that she had made for him so she could show him the plants in the garden. She let him touch the tomatoes, the corn and its shiny tassels, the pole beans and the Butternut squash, all the while saying their Dakota names. Anxiously awaiting his first words, she laughed when he said, "Ana.." with a lisp. While she held him and sat on the chair a friend of Casmir had hewn out of a log, she would point to the birds and wild fowl, geese and ducks and show how various they were. As the sun was setting behind her and sent rays over the waters, she brought him to the river bank and sang lullabies to him.

"Canta waste

hoksila ake istima

Good-hearted boy

go back to sleep

Hanhepi ki waste

The night is good."

One morning when she carried him into the living room she noticed movement across the street. "Look! Who are they?" She brushed back his dark hair and held him with her at the front window framed by chintz curtains while she gazed at the newcomers moving into her family's old homestead. A young couple with a boy and two younger girls were carrying belongings from a cart. Their mother was lean and haggard and glanced about the neighborhood with anxiety while her sturdy husband seemed to be pleased that they had a home. They were all dressed in drab brown clothing of coats and cloaks and caps and scarves.

"We must find out who they are," Anya said, peering into Stanley's steel blue eyes which gave her a chill every time. He was growing more and more into the image of his father, and she wondered how long she could endure that.

While the infant slept in the cradleboard she made for him, she would iron or darn clothes and reminisce, missing the feasts of the planting and of the harvest and the preparations for winter that her tribe followed, caught up in the movement of the seasons, each of them a celebration in its own right. The harvest celebrations lasted for days in which her heart beat with the drumming and the ululations while they-circle danced around the fire and feasted on savory buffalo meat. In the spring, they honored the seeds and seedlings and small game; in the summer, the rich, bountiful forests of food, and in the fall, the plentiful harvest. Now instead, Anya was expected to participate in All Saints Eve of the church, the Thanksgiving that President Lincoln had proclaimed, and the festivities of Christmas, New Year, and Easter.

She thought it strange that Europeans honored their ancestors, their saints and holy souls, on one day of the year while she honored her ancestors who dwelled with her every day.

Thanksgiving she passed off as a strange misunderstanding of the Wampanoag feast of thanks at the abundant harvest, a celebration that could go on for days, even weeks with dancing, storytelling, trading of goods while food, though enjoyed, was almost an afterthought.

Christmas was an entirely new experience. That winter, approaching the time when the sun was furthest from the earth, she heard a thumping at the back door, which she rushed to open. Casmir burst in dragging a medium sized, snow encrusted pine tree. Down the hall, past the kitchen, dining room and into the living room he went, leaving a streak of melting snow and the fragrance of the fallen evergreen needles behind him. With her help, he hoisted the tree into a holder where it stood near the entrance to the front room. Breathing hard with exertion, he stomped upstairs and returned with a large box full of decorations, while directing her to retrieve the other box, which contained the Christmas crèche. He then retreated to the kitchen for a snack and some tea while she proceeded to decorate the tree and lay out the crèche.

Inspired by the angel crowned tree, it's baubles and covered candles, lit into the night, she savored the smell of pine pitch which she also would have experienced while sitting before the winter fires of her tiospaye; Anya knelt and fingered the figures of the crèche and thought about the strength of the small family where Mary had given birth in a manger. Later, recalling the scene with the gifts given in colorfully wrapped boxes, the festivities and songs, the feast made her heart glad. Even each of the nearby churches had its towering, festooned tree and large manger scene, surrounded by evergreen tree boughs, which carried the scent of the forests she once roamed. And always, at the end of the celebrations, the carolers arrived, sang and closed with the Polish National Anthem.

For two years, Anya endured her captivity, finding comfort in the company of the child she had born, not out of love, but necessity. Her loneliness would be alleviated at times by Casmir, who would come home from work, play with the child and talk with Anya about his problems at his job or with his in-laws. Rarely would Zeke be mentioned, and he seldom appeared in their lives. When he showed up at the annual feasts, he would stay in the company of men, who gathered together in groups to discuss politics.

35

CASMIR'S DEMANDS

Stanley was almost three when Casmir approached Anya about another child. It occurred one winter's night after a long celebration of Casmir's brother Andrew's birthday After they and their children had said goodnight, shuffled off to their carriage where they sat among their gifts, she had retreated, exhausted to her bed.

When she awoke in the dark, she felt Casmir, reclining next to her, fumbling with her nightgown. As she pushed him away and batted aside his eager hands, she muttered, half asleep, "No, Casmir. No!" A shock wave of realization coursed through her when he insisted and she tried to sit up.

"You don't understand. We are man and wife. You must submit!" He pushed her down and imposed himself on her. "This was supposed to be OUR bedroom, not just yours," he whispered in her ear.

He subdued her struggles with the considerable weight of his body and muffled her cries with a hard, wet kiss on her mouth while he pushed up her gown and plunged into her with a grunt. Hot tears streamed down her face as he thrust and cried out, "Oh Anya! My Anya!" When he was finished, he lay back on the pillow and sighed with satisfaction, his arms encircling her and his hands holding onto her breasts, which he slowly released as he fell into a deep slumber, marked by his gurgling snores.

Anya bared her teeth, untangled herself from his grasp, slipped out of bed, lifted the awakening child out of his crib, and made her way into the parlor where she sat on the overstuffed chair and fell asleep while cradling and suckling Stanley. At the crack of dawn, she awoke and looked up to see Casmir standing in front of her in his nightshirt.

"I did not agree to your assault," she said glaring into his defiant eyes, "I thought the wedding ceremony was done because you wanted to protect me, like a father safeguards his child."

"It was a wedding," he insisted, "Didn't you say 'I will' to becoming my wife?" He laughed. "You foolish girl, don't you know what a contract is? It's an honest agreement, and you must pay a price for it," he snarled.

"If it's so honest, then why do I feel defiled?" she moaned. "What kind of contract is it where you can do anything you want with me? Don't I have something to say about that? I didn't hear words like that during the ceremony – that I can't even be allowed a decent night's sleep, that you can come and go as you please, that you don't even have to get my consent or warn me.... " She broke off into deep, shivering sobs.

He shook his head and muttered incessantly, "It was a contract...I have rights," he repeated while he left to stomp up the stairs to his attic room to get ready for work and stomped down, grabbed food from the kitchen and departed with a hefty slam of the door.

Shortly afterwards, Anya arose, dressed and left in search of the hardware she needed and which she bought from the trading post in the small settlement. While returning, she held Stan's little hand and they walked together until he was too tired. As she carried him, she thought *she should have known better; she should have known that the wasi'chu would not give her anything for nothing – not even her much needed safe haven.* That afternoon, she installed the simple lock on her door, which she made fast every evening only to be awakened in the middle of the night by Casmir pushing against its bolt with his plaintive whining, "Please, Anya,"

36

BORN AGAIN

The tiny white silk embroidered gown was draped over Anya's arms while the living breathing bundle it enveloped moved, ever so slightly. Anya peeked at the infant's ruddy face under its baptismal cap, a face Anya named Dawn, but Casmir insisted was Sophia. "What does that mean?" she had asked.

He looked at her with astonishment, for he almost seemed to believe that she was the Polish Tatar woman he had invented. "It means wisdom," he said.

"Wisdom," Anya savored the word, glancing up at Casmir. "But she's not old enough to show wisdom."

"What difference does that make?" he responded petulantly. "Anyway, it was my mother's name. You don't seem to mind Stan. And Jana is a good godmother for him."

"Oh," Anya recalled the stories he had told her about his mother in Poland, how she had helped him to become the bookkeeper he was here at the mills.

They sat in silence for awhile in the carriage Casmir had rented to take them to old St. Adalbert's Church in St. Paul for the baptism. "My mother passed away years ago in Posnan, Poland." He looked at her out of the corner of his eye and then laughed. "I forgot that we were never formally introduced. We're just a lucky match" She recoiled. *Lucky for you, maybe,* she thought and peeked at the baby once more.

"There's an old Hebrew belief," Casmir said. "If you are named after someone in your family, that person will escort you to heaven on the Last Day."

"Maybe I should give her my name then." Anya held the infant close to her breast. "I will never let any harm come to this child." *And I would gladly escort her along the trail of stars*, she thought while settling the infant in her arms as the carriage traveled the rugged roads.

They were greeted at the church by the godparents, Casmir's brother and sister-in-law, Andrew and Constance, who were dressed in the smartest fashion of the time, she in her blue silk dress with an ornately decorated square neck and an elaborate bustle, indicating that it must have been imported; and he, in a dark suit with a collarless waistcoat, a narrow tie, a wide collared coat, squared shoes and a top hat. Just as Jana and Dr. Kasminski were godparents to Stanley, these two strangers, who lived miles away in Winona, were supposed to oversee the parenting of Sophia.

Constance, tossed her small head, covered with a feathered cap over henna curls surrounding her shrewd looking face and Andrew fidgeted with his waistcoat chain. Both of them seemed to want to get the ceremony over with quickly. *The baptism would take far too long for them*, Anya thought while lifting the sleeping baby up and over into Constance's waiting arms. The infant fidgeted, indicating that she might object to a new, heavily perfumed presence.

"Do you renounce Satan? And all his works and pomps?" the priest asked Anya's little Dawn while the rest of them answered in unison for her, "I do." The priest's voice droned on while Anya's mind wandered. During Stanley's baptism, she had thought the priest was referring to Zeke as Satan. Who was he referring to now? Casmir? She glanced at him. After he became aware that she was pregnant again, he left her alone, which to her was a blessed relief. But then, he may want another child, she thought, while dread crept through her body like a chill in the wind.

She watched with numbed awe while the holy oil was signed with a cross on the infant and salt was placed on the infant's tongue, indicating strength and steadfastness. Then came the most significant moment of all – when the priest poured the waters over the head of her child, *the living waters, Anya thought, remembering the coursing surge of the river, its mighty life-giving waters enriched by the melting snows and the rains from the heavens, the water without which nothing could live.* The waters were poured over her child's head and she was baptized with her name, Sophia, the temple of her body enshrined forever, like the child Jesus, in the loving Spirit of God, who existed like a living fountain of love within.

On the return home, she was relieved to notice that Casmir was still concerned about her stamina when he assisted her from the carriage and guided her into the house where Mrs. Wisniewski presided over the celebration with cake, coffee and tea. Jana was caregiver this time, and Casmir's brother and his wife with their children were there, giving Stanley ample opportunity to play with friends, other than Jana's children. Their voices and laughter rang out and ringed the building, bringing a smile to Anya's lips. But Casmir took that as a sign of weariness and hurriedly ushered Anya into her room with the infant. She sat on a rocking chair he had placed near the bed and nursed the newborn Sophia while listening to snatches of conversation on the other side of the door. Casmir was defending her Tatar ancestry, and she noticed that he had hid her cradleboards behind the bed.

"She is, you know, delicate, like Anna," he said.

"She looks pretty strong to me," retorted Constance with her sharp edged voice.

"And she does not look at all Polish, Spanish maybe, or even Italian," Andrew added, in a gruff, nasal undertone. "She didn't seem all that attentive during the ceremony," he added. "What kind of Christian mother will she be? She looks so dark and pagan."

Casmir laughed, betraying his nervousness. "You remember the schoolbooks we had once, Andrew? Showing the Tatar invasion? Remember the drawings of the dark Tatars?"

"Oh what does it matter now, you're married and she is the mother of two of your children." Mrs Wisniewski's shrill voice broke into the conversation. "One thing I know for sure is that she's much too shy; stays off by herself and tries to avoid me every chance she gets. I have never once seen her in a conversation with a neighbor, never."

"And what about her Muslim background?" Constance continued, not letting go of the subject of Anya if she could help it.

"Oh that," Casmir chuckled, "Father Pietrowski gave her good instructions, baptized her, the works. She's a good Catholic now."

"Hmm, I would like to have a talk with her about that. She didn't join in much at the recitations during the ceremony." Constance retorted.

"Maybe she did not understand; she's new, you know." Casmir's voice trailed off. At her question about Anya's age, he answered, "Oh I think about nineteen.

"Ah, and so young," Andrew said, standing and fetching his and his wife's wraps. "At that age you never know how irresponsible they'll be."

"I tell you, Casmir, you are going to have trouble with her someday." Constance took her wrap and opened the door to call to her children.

"Oh no, she's a good mother, so attentive and gentle." Casmir arose to say goodbye while Mrs. Wisniewski opened the bedroom door and motioned for Anya to come out and see them off. Anya wrapped the baby tightly and held her close as if she were shielding the child against the shallow, nasty woman who was now Sophia's "godmother." They left in a hurry, having said, goodbye, they turned, boarded the carriage, and Andrew urged the horses down the dark street.

37

NEWCOMERS

The deep river reflected the golden sun of autumn which Anya showed Stan and Sophie. "Look," she said, while holding Sophie and letting go of Stan's hand as they stood upon the embankment in the vacant lot next to the old cabin. "See the ripples over there, and there. That's fish coming to the surface."

"Hello. And who are you?" a young man's voice wafted over the meadow.

Anya turned to see the new owner of the old cabin, a young, yet sandy haired gentleman, who looked at her curiously while he strode over to stand beside her. "My name is Stephen Jurwati," he said. "I'm the owner of this land."

Anya smiled at the incongruity, owning the land that he had never bought, but had, in essence, taken from Griswald and, ultimately, her family, her nation. She complied, giving him her name and introducing him to her children. He seemed kind and gentle, a good man. She watched his eyes light up when he told her about his three children, Joseph, Stephanie, and Lana. His wife was recuperating, he said, from the harrowing trip from Poland. "The food and accommodations on the ship were terrible," he said, shoving his hands into his pockets and scanning the flow of the river. "Mary, my wife, and I thought we were going to die. Seas churned waves to hundreds of feet above us, but the captain maneuvered the ship around them. We, almost lost everything we ever owned; our cabins, our supplies were soaked with briny waters. The ship was even listing when it arrived at the New York Port. We arrived from Krakow, and I wonder how my relatives and friends from Warsaw fared on their ships to Canada."

But he was glad they had made the trip, for there was good work at the mills and they were doing well. He had met Casmir and he liked the neighborhood. His wife, Mary, appreciated living among Polish people. "It is like a little Poland for her," he said.

"You have a slight accent when you speak Polish," he added. "Is it true, that you are from the Steppes? A Tatar?"

So her reputation had preceded her, she thought. Anya smiled again, rocked little Sophie back and forth in her arms, and said nothing. She detested the lie, but realized that she had to live with it. "I must go now," she said, grasping Stan's hand and turning toward Casmir's home. "It's getting late and I need to make supper"

"Oh the reason why I asked is that I think there are some Tatars on my side of the family, too," he continued blithely, disregarding her discomfort.

"Really? You don't look like one," she retorted while she glanced at his deep blue eyes and light brown hair.

"But you should see my wife," he responded, as she walked away. He seemed to want to continue the conversation, but she had had enough of the lie.

The days that followed were filled with a routine that Anya found tedious, her only respite being the garden and her close companionship with the children. Casmir was becoming more and more amorous, but she managed to demurely turn him away at the bedroom door with a gentle, "Not just yet, dear Casmir." Living in their rows of boxed in houses, the neighbors seemed to find a catharsis in petty disputes and mean spirited gossip that Anya found unbearable.

One afternoon, following the long walk to the town and just before she entered the corner store, her heart jumped at the sight of a decorated white horse hitched to a nearby post. *Dakota paintings,* she thought, while examining the sun rays and lightning bolts under its forelock and around its eyes. While resting Sophie on her hip and guiding Stan in front of her, she touched the stunning horse who lifted his head and whinnied. A decorated pinto was hitched next him. Though she rarely entered the trading post, since it was, more or less, a meeting place for men who also bought their hunting and fishing gear there; she pushed open the door.

Standing at the counter with their backs to her were two Dakotas. One of them turned to glance at her, but did a double take.

She backed out the door and waited for him. "Tokala Kohana!" she said softly, restraining her joy when he walked out the door and saw her. "Anpaytoo!" They both carefully approached each other so that they would not attract attention.

He touched her on the shoulder and looked down at Sophie. "What's this?"

"A lot has happened since you left," she said, pressing her hand against his and speaking in a voice barely above a whisper. "We must be cautious," she said, "for even the walls have ears." Then, casually, she looked away while saying, "This is Casmir's and my child, Sophie."

"Old man Casmir?" He stared at her with disbelief. His young face had changed and had become weather beaten and worn. His buckskin was ragged and soiled, and he carried the smell of tobacco and sweat with him even though his hair was meticulously plaited into one long black braid with a headband and feather, as was his friend's.

"And this is Stan. You can guess who his father is." She grabbed Tokala Kohana's head and whispered fiercely into his ear and drew back. "But don't tell the boy. He doesn't know."

He gave her a baffled look. "So you're all settled in here, then?"

"Settled? Oh no! Not at all, Tokala Kohana." Her eyes were filled with desperation. "Did you not hear me, Tokala? I have been…."

He nodded.

"Anpaytoo, I want you to meet our medicine man, Howahkan" he turned and looked at his friend, a fierce looking, statuesque Dakota, many years older than Tokala, who had followed him out of the trading post and was standing behind him. Howahkan gestured toward the children and then stared at Anya.

Tokala Kohana gestured at Anya and responded in Dakota, "My sister, Anpaytoo, here, was introduced to her womanhood," he turned and looked directly into the holy man's eyes. "the was'ichu's way."

A light of recognition crossed Howahkan's eyes as he grimaced and then nodded his head in assent. Tokala Kohana turned to her with a face that beamed like the sun and said, "Then we need to take you back with us. How soon can you be ready?"

38

THE ESCAPE (1880)

The clouds parted around the waning moon that morning, while Anpaytoo breathed in the scent of buds breaking open from the trees and undergrowth. The bundled infant at her breast sighed, her tiny chest rising and falling in sweet contentment, while the little boy in his blue shirt, tucked into his breeches, at her side struggled to stay awake, his eyes closing and his head nodding until he leaned against her, fast asleep. Seated at the back of the narrow wagon on sheaves of hay, Anpaytoo, in her traditional Dakota dress, felt like singing.

The two Dakota men had traded for the wagon from a friend and hitched it to their horses. While they sat conversing on the driver's seat, their voices sounded as indistinct as the low murmur of bees. Anpaytoo knew they were discussing the route, whether it was wise to travel away from the river route to their former Dakota village campsite. But she had wanted to show Tokala Kohana the graves so they could send their cries to Tasunke Paytah, Takota Wachinskapa, and Makawee Hantaywee, calling to them in the spirit world. Tokala Kohana also needed to know that their deaths were respected in the Dakota way.

"This is a heavy burden," he had said when in town she had told him about their passing.

He had stared past the buildings and into a space beyond. "So they killed Paytah with their dirty water and the others?" She lowered her head, indicating that she did not know. He held his fist to his heart and turned away so she would not see the agony in his eyes. "We must go to them and honor them together," he had said. For now, though, Anpaytoo and the children dozed off, moving gently with the cart as if on a small boat traveling up river.

Anpayto, is this it? Is this the place?" They had stopped and Tokala Kohana was shaking her awake. Her eyes opened and met with the blinding sunlight behind his face, a shadow in front of it, until she turned and carefully placed Sophie in her cradleboard and slid down from the cart. Stanley scrambled awkwardly down after her. What she saw was not the forest of scaffolds in sacred burial grounds, but houses, a cluster of houses.

She looked around for the markers of the camp – the two tall birches at the lakeside. They were there, as she had last noticed when she discovered her parent's grave sites. But at that time, the settlers had built only as far as the outskirts. She whirled around in bewilderment. "It can't be…" She stared at the buildings aghast. "But Wicasa was guarding it; he said settlers were afraid to go there, and even Casmir thought it was haunted."

"Well, it's gone now," said Tokala Kohana's companion, Howahkan, in his deep baritone. "That explains it." He and Tokala exchanged knowing glances. "They probably ransacked the place and took whatever they found to their museums." He looked into her stunned face. "They do that, you know. Collect parts of us, like souvenirs that they study behind counters of glass at their museums or, even worse, their pawn shops."

"But what is it that it explains?" Anpaytoo asked Howahkan.

"We heard hunting party reports that Wicasa was seen among the Lakotas out west,".

Tokala Kohana had to restrain Anpaytoo, who let out an agonizing wail. He held her close and whispered, "My sister, there is nothing we can do. Let us have a mourning ceremony with our tiospaye in Canada." There was a stirring in the houses, and so he guided her and the child, Stan, back onto the wagon. "Let's go!" he said, leaping onto the driver's seat next to Howahkan who clicked the reins urging the horses onward at a steady gait. To see the gravesite, they had gone too far out of their way. They all knew that each moment of delay was crucial.

At the city limits, they stopped and Tokala Kohana jumped down, cut a large branch from a sycamore tree and used it to brush away their tracks. At each stop, the two men unhitched and mounted their horses in order to backtrack with tree branches to sweep away signs of their trail. During the miles that followed, Anpaytoo wept, sobbed and moaned, even in her sleep;

yet they moved onward with pain in their eyes, crimped from weeping. They drove on, endlessly.

While driving through St. Cloud, they came to a halt in order to feed, water and rest the horses, and they tarried at the town's outskirts on a rise near the Mississippi River. At the overlook, they saw that the harbor was crowded with massive steamships and quaint paddleboats in the rippling, sparkling, placid river. Women in their rustling silk gowns with elaborate bustles protruding behind them carried their parasols and small cases in gloved hands as they walked up the wide plank to the decks of the steamships. Some wore black, others in bright blue or scarlet with contrasting deep blue or green velvet paneled fronts. With their jewelry glinting in the sunlight, they were a colorful sight. Many had brightly feathered bonnets perched on top of their upswept curls. Some stood on the deck at the rail of the ship with their husbands, both of them waving to relatives and friends below as they prepared to travel south down the great Mississippi to St. Louis or New Orleans.

Having watched them from afar, Anpaytoo seemed to be distracted from her shock over the loss of the sacred cemetery grounds. The people below seemed harmless enough, living the lives which were customary for them. She wanted to stay there for awhile and take hold of her heart, beating against the wall of fear her mind was beginning to build. *What would people want with the remains of our loved ones, if not the complete removal of our existence? The tiospaye would have nothing to remember our people by, nothing, not even a stone in the ground nor a scaffold in the sky*, she thought. Her sense of forboding plunged deep, and she became determined to stay away from these people, attractive and yet so full of evil trickery. As she watched them, engrossed in their own lives, she knew they would never understand her.

Relentless, the small group of Dakotas moved on, pursuing their immediate goal to stop near the Sauk River tributary where they would pitch camp at nightfall near the refreshing rapids. When they arrived at the riverside location, the entire party was grimy from the long trip through dusty winds over muddy roads. The site was once occupied at various times by Ottawa, Ojibwe and the Winnebago (Ho Chunk) until their treaty opened the entire area to settlers. Since then, the town's people had mined granite quarries that could be seen along the river banks. The forelorn travelers wandered among the weeping willows, stately oaks, elms and silver maple and came upon a tamarack bog, filled with rosemary, Labrador tea, bog laurel, and early low blueberry, hummocks of sphagnum moss and cotton grass sedges.

"Tamarack is the only pine tree that turns golden in the fall and drops its needles," said Howkahtan while exploring the hummock with them.

Anpaytoo ventured into the herb layer where she harvested crested shield fern, tussock cotton-grass, rusty cotton-grass, white meadowsweet, steeplebush, cinnamon fern, royal fern, bog, St. John's wort, and flat-topped aster. Like her mother, she stored these herbs and tamarack needles and bark in burlap bags for future medicinal use.

As she sat near the campfire that evening, the reflections of its flames glimmering in her eyes; she saw to it that Sophia was well fed and fast asleep in her cradleboard. Stan, her little boy she often called Fierce Storm, was listening to stories that Howahkan was telling him.

"Wi is the sun up there that you see in the daytime, and Hanwi is the night sun, that is called the moon." Howkahtan explained. "Skan, the sky-chief, was angry with Wi for leaving his wife, Hanwi, during a festival, and so Skan made Wi rule over the day and Hanwi, over the night. Wohpe, their daughter, is the White Buffalo Woman."

Stan's head was thrown back as he looked up at the moon with his eyes full of wonder. "Wi, Hanwi, Wohpe," he repeated with his childish lisp, then bent his head down, grabbed a stick and began to scribble in the dirt where he was sitting. Howkahtan laughed, gently poked him, and watched him giggle. Then he fed him a spoonful of stew from the cooking pot.

"The steamship passengers wore fancy clothes and could have anything they wanted," Tokala Kohana commented on the busy scene they had watched. "Do you miss that kind of life, Anpaytoo?"

"Never!" Anpaytoo looked up and glared at him. "Don't ever think that of me. It feels good to be Dakota again, and, besides, I was uncomfortable in their outfits," she said, while seated with them around the campfire and lifting a piece of rabbit meat from the cooking pot to her lips. "If you can imagine what it feels like to wear a corset with steel braces, covered with heavy silk, you will agree with me. Besides, old man Casmir called me Anya and told them that I was a Tatar from the steppes of Poland."

"A Tatar?" asked Tokala Kohana.

"I do not know what that is, but I had to smile and nod my head every time his daughter-in-law asked me what it felt like to be a Muslim." She shook her head. "I'd rather die a thousand deaths than live their lies about me. Here, it may seem like a hard life, but it lets me know who I really am. Without knowing that, I am truly a lost one." She captured the meat in her mouth and savored it while she consumed it, ladling the vegetable laden soup into a wooden bowl.

"A Muslim?" Tokala Kohana paused to reflect, his finely chiseled face, weather-beaten from enduring the earth's elements. "You've had many names, Anpaytoo. How did you know which one to answer to?"

"I will always know I am, Anpaytoo HanWi, the Light of the Sun, the sacred name that hides behind theirs."

"The wasi'chus set snares for us, you know. We are often caught up in the trap of their lies, and we must be cautious so that we will not lose ourselves in them." said Howahkan.

"It's good to know that I am only one person, Anpaytoo, the Dakota. I can feel Wakan Tanka in this place even though the priest drilled me in their Christian religion with their God on the cross. I wept for him, for I could feel his terrible pain. But they hung the cross in their homes and churches and did not understand what he endured, just as they do not understand the sufferings of their sick and poor. They'd walk by, not even noticing Christ on the cross nor those who were begging them for their help. They even hit their children who were looking for their guidance." She looked pensively into the fire. "I've never known a more hard-hearted people than the white man."

39

IN ENEMY TERRITORY

Following the Mississippi River Trail for several days was a tedious journey through what seemed like never ending flat lands. On the way, they passed through River Falls where settlers were busy filling in a ravine which sent the overflow from nearby Fletcher Creek into the Mississippi. The work puzzled the travelers, for they had accepted the wisdom of letting the earth regulate the pulse and direction of her streams.

"They are working – like many ants," laughed Howahkan, "building a town on a chasm."

The Dakotas watched with amusement while the settlers labored, filling up the cavern.

After setting up camp that evening, Anpaytoo walked away from the birch, pine and oak trees along the river and opened her arms wide to greet the prairie and the sun, descending along the western horizon. It was as if she held the painted sky in a frame formed by her heart and soul. The colors – amber, purple and vermilion — seemed to spill over the vast grasslands and onto her decorated deerskin. Under the shimmering light, the prairie seemed to undulate, like waves in an ocean of tall grass and wildflowers.

While scattering a handful of tobacco, she uttered her prayer to Wakan Tanka in the four directions, turned to the West, abode of the power of the Thunderbird where the sun goes down, turned to the North, place of the bald-eagle, where Waziah's lodge sends purifying winds, turned to the East, path of the long-winged, rising sun which brings light (Hunka), the source of wisdom and knowledge, and finally turned to the South where all living things thrive. She caught her breath when a Golden Eagle screamed and flew overhead, making her communion with the Great Mystery complete.

Rushing back to camp, her eyes flashing over cheeks flushed with excitement, she told them, "Do you see how the prairie looks like sunlit waves? I never thought I'd see the day when I would be free again, when I would be able to hold this land and sky in my arms as ours again, to know that we belong here together forever."

"You were wandering, lost on the dark path of difficulties, until my path crossed yours and, when we met, you chose my red road instead – that was sacred," said Tokala Kohana.

Howahkan stood up and took both her hands. His coal black eyes of wisdom engaged hers, seeking answers, and he said, "You have been on a hard journey, but, even though you may not have felt it, you were not alone. We sang over you in our hearts daily, for many winters. Yours was a long *Ishna Ta Awi Cha Lowan.*" He would never forget the look of sheer gratitude in her eyes at that moment. When she made ready for a night's sleep, the moon peered from behind clouds in the darkness, as if she had covered the stars, '*like children under a blanket*,' Anpaytoo thought

When the dawn broke, they resumed their trek onward and noticed that the four legged life around them was becoming more plentiful. Deer seemed to abound as did bobcats and wolves. A black bear and her cubs appeared in and out of the tall grass in the distance and a moose with its large, broad rack trudged across the marshlands. "This is prime land for grouse and pheasants," said Tokala Kohana, marveling at their sightings of abundant game.

As they pitched camp, Howahkan explained that they were at a former Ojibwey settlement, but the white man had come there to build a town for the railroad, its bridge spanning the wide Mississippi in a city the railroad president named Brainerd.

"It was the place of the 'Blueberry Wars,'" said Howahkan. "According to a legend, the Ojibwey Chief brought the white settlers of the town a peace offering of a blueberry pie even though they had hung two of his braves and had brought with them the feared 'Iron Horse.' The story shows that we natives are peaceful people. But the white man only sees another side of us, our fierce love for the land."

That evening the travelers heard a pack of wolves howling in unison, fading in and out, distant and yet near and responding to each other like a a chorus in harmony. At nightfall, they lay in their blankets around the campfire, the children in the hay-filled wagon in their cradleboards, covered with netting against the mosquitoes. Heavy sticks made into pitch-fired torches surrounded their camps while on this clear night, Anpaytoo lay, face up, staring at the galaxies of stars overhead. They were so big she felt that she could reach up and capture them. She located the Pole Star,(*Wichapi Owanjila the star that stays in one place),* also known as the North Star, one of the Maghpia Oyate (Cloud People), who still broods over the loss of his Lakota spouse, Tupun Shawin (the Red-Cheeked Maid), who fell through the clouds when she tried to dig up a plant there. Anpaytoo was prepared to await the appearance of Tupun Shawin's son, Fallen Star, who returned to the Maghpia Oyate and would appear in the morning. She smiled over this legend she remembered from the many Wicasa had told her when they lived within the Dakota nation before the tribe left for Canada and her tiospaye stayed behind with graying, gaunt and lonely Troubled Spirit.

At daybreak, Anpaytoo awoke to Tokala Kohana's excited cries, "Look!" He shouted while he ran up the riverbank after his morning preparations and grabbed his rifle. Howahkan joined him and both scanned the skies over the land where geese spread out for miles, heading north. By the time Anpaytoo stood up and tended to the awakening children; the sky was blackened with flying Canadian geese. "Look!" She, herself, cried out and Stan echoed back in his thin child's voice, "Look!"

Stanley toddled out into the thick prairie grass where he fell onto some burs and brambles. His face wrinkled with an anguished cry, and Anpaytoo stooped to pick him up and return to Sophia in her cradleboard.

"There, there, good little boy," she murmured while removing the burs. Four rifle shots resounded in the air, and she turned to see Tokala Kohana and Howahkan wading through the tall grass to fetch their fallen prey.

"Didn't even make a dent in that crowd," Howahkan exclaimed when he and Tokala Kohana returned, carrying their two geese apiece, holding them high. "We have more meat for dinner now." Tokala Kohana admired the geese, fattened by wintering down south.

Alternating their meals with grouse and pheasants from the prairies and bass, walleye and trout from the great river and its streams; they filled their gourds with pure, sweet water to quench their thirst. While Stanley wandered naked into a stream, caught minnows with his cupped hands and laughed with delight; they waded into the waters to cleanse their bodies, and Anpaytoo dug up roots from the land and gathered herbs and berries, for savory scented stews.

They broke camp to continue for days on their long journey as far as the town of Lake Bemidji, near the end of their trail, which was the beginning of the meandering source of the wide and mighty Mississippi. "No one really knows where the Mississippi River starts," said Howahkan, surveying the lake country before them and pointing to the smaller lakes and streams nearby. "The Minnesota and the Mississippi Rivers seem to be like relatives, feeding each other and joining together further on downstream, until they part." He grew silent at the sight of others among the trees, for he was well aware that this was Ojibwey territory, the land of their enemies.

"Tokala Kohana!" he called and together the two talked about the risks they were taking.

That evening, Tokala Kohana told Anpaytoo that he and Howahkan were going to perform a "coup" on the Ojibway. They would tell them what they could about why they were there, but at the same time, approach them, maybe even shake hands. Seeking news of a party of white men which may be in desperate pursuit, Tokala Kohana and Howahkan entered the town nearby and walked into the nearest saloon. In the shadows that the gaslight played on their features, they leaned against the bar and ordered a few drinks, looking over their shoulders for friendly Indians. One Ojibwey arose from a table where he and some others were playing cards and walked toward them. Standing next to Howahkan, he asked," Don't you know that it's dangerous for Sioux to show their faces here in Minnesota?

"When has it ever not been dangerous?" Howahkan replied.

"But there's a price on your heads, not that it matters to us."

"We came here to bring back those who had been left behind," interjected Tokala

Kohana, "my mother, father, brother and sister. The only one who survived was my sister with two mixed blood children, made the wasi'chu's way with our women."

"We do not plan to stay. We are just passing through to Grandmother's Land. (Canada)" Howahkan said in his deep baritone voice.

The Ojibwey looked down and grunted, then eyed Tokala Kohana. "I know that if I had two mixed blood children that someone came and took. I would not rest until I found them."

Howahkan nodded. "That's why we're here. Have you heard about such a search party?"

The Ojibwey shook his head. "No, but I think, if I were them, the first place I'd go would be out west, into Lakota country where most of the Sioux went after the uprising, not here in enemy territory."

"Good." Hawahton nodded. "I was thinking the same way. That gives us time for our trail to grow cold." Much relieved, he shoved both their drinks over to the Ojibway and motioned for Tokala Kohana to leave.

After their brief stay near Bemidji, they moved on about a day's journey further north to stop at a pristine area. "Listen to the noise of this Elk Lake," Hawahton said, leaning towards it.

"It's like music," said Anpaytoo. "And listen," she added gesturing upward at the incessant bird song in the air.

"So much life-force is here that a white man gave it another name, Itasca, which means 'True Source.' But we still don't know, the real beginnings of the great rivers, for this whole area used to be one huge, glacial lake," Howahkan said with a sweeping motion of his arm.

Gigantic fir timber stands arose in front of them, casting shaggy reflections into the waters, while the land behind them was filled with hardwood trees that tossed their leafy branches in the windswept air. Having found the meandering, northwestward path through the woods toward Rainy River which followed the border between the U.S. and Canada; they planned to make camp, but the two braves both looked at the inviting waters, then at each other, and ran a few paces where they tossed off their loin cloths and dashed whooping into the lake. Anpaytoo, carried little Sophia in her cradleboard to the edge of the lake, while guiding Stanley there with her other hand. She stripped little Stan and let him frolic in the waves while she lifted up Sophia, naked, and dipped her into the lake for a cleansing. She wiped down both of them with a soft cloth and bundled them in their colorful woolen blankets.

Refreshed and dressed in loin cloths with their long black hair in braids, the two braves returned to set up a tipi for a longer stay than usual. The two men lifted the heavy poles and Anpaytoo wrapped white deerskin around the structure. Howahkan made sure that the entrance faced east and then honored the tipi, blessing it with smoke from his sacred pipe. He was a tall, imposing man with hair streaked with grey and rough hewn features, which he painted with streaks of red, yellow and black on moments such as these. He too, like Wicasa, wore a bear claw necklace when the occasion called for it. One, tall eagle feather was showing from the back of the band around his head, for he had reverently tucked away his war bonnet. Together, they dug the interior pit, filled it with logs and set the central fire, scattering it with sage, cedar and sweet grass. Howahkan lit his pipe with kinnikinnick and shared it with them as they sat around the sacred fire.

"Don't unwind too much," warned Anpaytoo. "You will need to be alert to danger."

"Don't worry, little sister," Tokala Kohana laughed. "The greatest danger is behind us."

"And we can be sure that we are safe," added Howahkan, passing around some of their supply of pemmican.

That afternoon, they whirled in a circle dance and chanted a song of thanks to all the winged creatures, two leggeds, four leggeds and fish who had fed them so far, but they stopped short when they saw in the distance a large elk standing near the lakeshore. "That's the leader of the herd," whispered Howahkan, putting one arm around Tokala Kohana, and the other around Anpaytoo. "He's checking out the place. See?" And sure enough, a herd of elk emerged from the forest behind their leader.

Just before evening fell, Tokala Kohana and Hawahkan returned to camp from a hunting foray, carrying the body of an elk trussed up on a large branch between them. "There's enough here to feed an entire tiospaye," Tokala Kohana exclaimed, while Anpaytoo thought of various uses for the hide, once she tanned it.

The following days were spent in exploring the bountiful life they were sharing with their elk relatives. Howahkan showed them the remains of the moraine where glaciers left deposits of silt, clay, gravel and sand as the great ice sheets moved on, leaving depressions behind them. Aspen, birch and red and white pine trees surrounded the lakes as did profuse growths of ram's-head lady's slippers, olivaceous spike-rush, bog adder's-mouth, slender naiad, and sheathed pondweed, with herbs that Anpaytoo conscientiously gathered. They heard the mournful call of loons, clacking noise of ducks, watched the grebes dive for food, and herons stalk the waters for their share. Vireos, tanagers, finches, kinglets, nuthatches, chickadees, and warblers made themselves heard, as the travelers watched an occasional cormorant's s deep dive and heard a woodpecker's incessant tapping. In a clearing they saw a bevy of hummingbirds feasting on wildflowers. In the night they heard the woo of the owl's call and whoosh of its flight in the darkness and the howls of a pack of grey wolves, who kept the abundance of white tailed deer in check. At daybreak, they even stumbled upon a sacred bald eagle's nest massive and high in a sturdy oak with its two ungainly fledglings. The adults were a sight to see, sweeping down from a great height and swooping up a bass or rainbow trout to feed their brood.

One evening, Tokala Kohana shared this story around the campfire. "When I left our tiospaye and went with the Dakota group who had made use of our ferry, we eventually rode further west on what they told me was a hunt. We were on great, vast empty plains when my horse began prancing with excitement, and I heard what sounded like rolling thunder. I looked up, but the skies were clear. The other members of the hunting party were scanning the distant horizon where I saw a thin black line that grew larger and larger until it became a gigantic dark ocean with waves and waves of buffalo right before my eyes. Like a flood, they covered the entire prairie and drummed up a storm of dust giving off a musky smell. They were heading straight toward us, and one of our party said to get our rifles ready for a great run. I shot one buffalo point blank and then rode along beside the others who shot their buffalo, one each. The buffalo were surrounding us, but parted to go past us while we jumped off our horses and dressed down the ones we killed."

Howahkan leapt up and with his hands held upward, shouted out, "Oh great Wankan Tankan, hear me! We send up our hearts with this kinnikinnic, send our thanks all around to the East, North, West, South, for your great abundance, for you and Mother Earth have cared for us from the beginning." They began a circle dance that lasted into the night with Howahkan using the sage smudge stick to bless them before they left the celebrations to find their sleeping cots.

40

HOMEWARD BOUND

After a few more days there and with a reluctant good-bye to the Elk Lake area, they dismantled the tipi and loaded their goods onto the wagon. After a long haul, they pulled up at the edge of Rainy River, deep, and wide, which lapped with placid waves against the shore until the life it held swirled to just beneath the surface. The woodlands that surrounded it, a mixture of oaks, birch, spruce and red pines, veiled the sunlight which broke in streams through the openings in the tall overhanging branches of their sanctuary. Set back and hidden in the undergrowth, wooden thatch houses of the Ojibway could be seen by glancing up the boardwalks that led to their docks on the riverbank.

After setting up camp with the tipi in a woodland opening, their first inclination was to cleanse themselves in the sparkling waters of Rainy River. Anpaytoo washed their clothes on the rocks upriver and hung them out to dry near the campfire. She swam in it and bathed herself, as well. The rest of the party swam nakedly and noisily downriver, laughing as they splashed in the refreshing waters. Wrapped in old, but colorful blankets, Anpaytoo with Sophie and the men and little boy, Stanley, sat around the fire in front of the tipi and ate the roasted river trout they had speared or caught with their bare hands while in the waters.

That evening, two members of the enemy tribe pushed a flatboat up to the landing near their campsite and stepped ashore through the muddy waters. "Who goes there?" One of them shouted.

"Dakotas! We come in peace!" Tokala Kohana and Howahkan shouted back in Ojibway. Wearing loin cloths, and while making signs of peace, they emerged from their makeshift tipi and headed toward their wagon. Hauling out kettles and blankets, they approached the two Ojibway tribesmen, who had painted fierce signs on their faces and bodies above their breech cloths. One of them looked long and hard at Howahkan's knife that he had sheathed at his side. After awhile, Howahkan unsheathed it and gave it to him. They took most of the kettles and the blankets on the wagon, nodded and departed with their goods piled high onto their flatbed boat.

"We will have a few days here," said Tokala Kohana when he returned triumphant to Anpaytoo where she was nursing Sophia in the tipi. "And we will have this to eat with our fish," He held up some squash and a large burlap bag of rice.

Howahkan looked bewildered. "But how will I clean the fish?"

"Better they use it on their fish than on you, my friend." Kohana laughed and clapped Howahkan on the shoulder. "Besides, we have more knives where that came from. Remember the ones we bought for my father and brother?" At that his voice caught in his throat, but he led his friend to the wagon where he pulled aside some buffalo robes that covered two knives, giving the one with the buffalo tusk handle to Howahkan.

The next morning, they waded and swam in the river, catching fish with some handmade nets and spears, until a good natured, though somewhat overweight, open-faced Ojibway named Good Eagle, wearing worn buckskin, paddled down in an outrigger, offered them another outrigger and directed them to follow him as he travelled upriver and portaged across a fiord to a hidden lake filled with walleye, pike, and small trout. When they emerged from under the thick stand of trees between the river and the lake, they were met with the expanse of water that Good Eagle, his rotund cheeks glowing under the glint of the sun and his full lips pulled back in a gap-toothed smile, called a "Sacred Gift". Its dark waters teemed with life and spread out for miles, yet remained hidden under the canopy of surrounding forest.

With spears and nets and even their bare hands, they filled their canoes with fish while little Stan giggled and squealed with delight. Anpaytoo, held Sophia in her cradleboard in Good Eagle's canoe, laughing with each splash of a catch. At one point, Tokala Kohana almost caught a gigantic walley, but the wily fish slipped out of his net at the last minute. *With elusive powers like that, no wonder it lived long enough to become a giant among its species,* thought Anpaytoo.

Their dugouts were low in the water after they trolled the lake, but they could not land at the area where they had traversed for they saw two black bear cubs on the shore by the tree stump where most of the fish were gutted. Like small dogs, standing on their hind legs, begging, the cubs pawed at the stump and its leftovers. Knowing that the mother bear was nearby, the party in their boats shouted and banged their gear together to frighten away her brood, who scampered away, disappearing in the nearby timber. When the party landed they abandoned the thought of preparing the fish there, but traversed in a hurry upriver where they paddled, pushing their heavy load back to their campsite.

Good Eagle helped them clean and prepare the fish, gathering up the unused parts in a burlap bag. "It's not good to have the scraps nearby. I know of a place to take them where the bears go." With that he left with the scraps.

But Tokala Kohana noticed that something else had gone with him. "Where's your new knife, Howahkan?" he asked.

"Good Eagle admired it." Howahkan replied.

Kohana laughed. "What else will they want?"

"I'm sure they'll let us survive," Anpaytoo joined in. "So that all of us can thank Wankan Tanka for what we have."

A few days later, as the receding forest revealed the glaring sun and further woodlands ahead, the party broke camp and continued on their journey. Traveling well into nightfall, the children were jostled to sleep in the rocking wagon. The travelers would awake the children, jump down, camp and then begin again before dawn. After what seemed like a repetitious, never ending quest in which they and the horses were worn and weary; one morning, the drivers spied the movement of a village near a lake ahead.

Adrift and drowsy, Anpaytoo was dreaming that she was lost on a forever moving stream with the tree branches and the underbrush closing in on her. From afar she heard, "Anpaytoo!" and the excitement in Tokala Kohana's voice roused her. She sat up in her crumpled doeskin dress, and, as she peered through the shafts of mid afternoon sunlight ahead, Anpaytoo's heart leapt for in the distance she saw Chayton Enapay in his best buckskin, standing tall and steadfast among the trees where he awaited their arrival. When he saw them, he mounted a magnificent black stallion and cantered toward them, his right hand held high in greeting.

"Ah ho!" he shouted and halted the horse, dismounted and held out his hands for Anpayto, who had already leapt from the wagon to run to him. Theirs was a close, heartfelt embrace.

"It's been so long," she murmured.

"Too long," he said, brushing back her hair, ragged from mourning, and holding her face, upturned in both his hands, looking deep into her eyes, he kissed her tenderly. Then he turned and placed Sable's reins into her hands and lifted her up onto the horse while he leapt up behind her. "Sable's yours now, he said. Before they cantered off, he noticed Howahkan and Kohana standing and leaning against their wagon, grinning.

At this point, the young woman closed her lap top so she could give her attention to the tattered second book that her great uncle Stanley wrote. Leather bound with tarnished gold clasps, the two books held his attempt at preserving the past, as he knew it, and to share his memories with future generations. The books were scratched and battered from years of travel, back and forth over many miles between Canada and both coasts of the United States; it was a wonder that they still existed to tell their tale. But when she found them among her mother's things after she died, the young woman cherished them, as if they were a treasure beyond belief.

Wiping the second book down with a well oiled cloth against the dusty leather cover, she put the cloth aside and gently opened the book. Its fragile pages revealed an incisive, yet, at times, looped hand writing, slanting upward with excitement at times, and downward, dark with sadness at other times. Some pages were blotched and illegible; others were clear with the driving purpose that her great uncle must have had. Though she wore soft, cotton gloves when she touched them, the pages sometimes shriveled and fell apart, a tragedy she tried to remediate by piecing the page together, taking a photo (since the page would be further damaged by tape or glue)and using the photo, itself, as the page.

To be sure, it was a tedious task, but she felt it was worth it. Rarely was her ancestors' past told with the close, personal attention of the son of her great grandmother. The reality of vigorous people living on a rich continent under siege could not have been more striking. How else could she have known that her great grandmother, was not a "squaw" to be abused by wisa'chu? That she was not the meaningless Anya, but the brilliant, beautiful Anpaytoo HanWi, "Light from the Sun," a Wisdom Keeper of the sacred red road, whose life with her tiospaye would enlighten the second book.

BIBLIOGRAPHY

Black Elk. *The Sacred Pipe: The Seven Rites of the Oglala Sioux. ("He Haka Sapa").* Edited and recorded by Joseph Epes Brown. University of Oklahoma Press, Norman OK, 1953.

Brown, Dee. *Bury My Heart at Wounded Knee: An American Indian History of the American West.* Henry Holt Owl Book Edition (1990), copyright, 1970, p.40.

Chomsky, Carol. *United States Dakota War Trials: A Study In Military Injustice.* University of Minnesota Law School Scholarship Repository, 1990.

Densmore, Frances. *Songs of the Sioux.* Library of Congress, 1951.

Dunbar Ortiz, Roxanne. *An Indigenous Peoples' History of the United States: Revisioning American History.* Beacon Press, 2014.

Horowitz, Tony. "The Horrific Sandcreek Massacre Will Be Forgotten No More." *Smithsonian Magazine,* 2014.

McDermott, Annette. *What Really Happened at the Battle of Little Big Horn?* www.History.com.

Paige, Henry W., PhD. *Songs of the Teton Sioux.* Westernlore Press, 1970.

1862 Dakota Let Them Eat Grass www.youtube.com.

Printed in the United States
By Bookmasters